Three sisters. One wedding. It'd be enough to drive anybody crazy.

NEELY: Reliable, hardworking, pragmatic...and single. That is until new beau Robert suddenly pops the question. Neely's as stunned as the rest of her opinionated Southern family. But she'd rather drink warm ice tea before introducing Robert to *that* clan.

SAVANNAH: Suburban, almost-empty-nester Savannah is having the mother of all midlife transformations. Sure, she's still gorgeous, married to a doctor and a whiz in the kitchen. But lately she's just been feeling so darn *invisible*. Only one way to change that...

VI: What's going on with the Mason family? Composed Neely is cracking jokes, Savannah has lost her perky glow and Vi...well, infuriating, eccentric, contrary baby-girl Vi is actually making sense for once. Could it be she's finally growing up?

Tanya Michaels

Tanya Michaels enjoys writing about love, whether it's the romantic kind or the occasionally exasperated affection we feel for family members. Tanya made her debut with a 2003 romantic comedy, and her books have been nominated for awards such as *Romantic Times BOOKclub*'s Reviewer's Choice, Romance Writers of America's RITA® Award, the National Readers' Choice and the Maggie Award of Excellence. In 2005, she won the prestigious Booksellers' Best Award. She's lucky enough to have a hero of a husband, as well as family and friends who love her despite numerous quirks. Visit www.tanyamichaels.com to learn more about Tanya and her upcoming books, or write to her at PMB #97, 4813 Ridge Road, Suite 111, Douglasville, GA 30134.

The
GOOD KIND
OF CRAZY

TANYA MICHAELS

In honor of my sister and dear friend, Lara Spiker

So this is what it feels like to be the unpredictable one in the family. A definite first for Neely Mason. One of four siblings, forty-five-year-old Neely was known for being reliable, hardworking, pragmatic…and single, much to the chagrin of her cheerfully opinionated Southern relatives.

But running the risk of becoming a sixty-year-old unwed cat lady had been Neely's sole nod toward eccentricity; it was her twenty-six-year-old sister, Vidalia, who habitually caught people off guard. Vi had been a surprise from the moment Mrs. Mason learned that her "early menopause" was actually a pregnancy. The unexpected late-in-life baby had grown into a quirky career student who still delighted in startling others. For a change, Vi's pretty bow-shaped mouth was hanging open in the same gape as everyone else's.

Ten minutes ago, the clank of silverware had been the background music to Savannah fussing that everyone got enough to eat and Douglas charming their parents with the latest anecdote starring Douglas. Now, silent shock was as tangible in the dining room as the heirloom mahogany furniture and the brass antique chandelier—the one Neely had always thought looked like a spider with lightbulb feet. Though rarely fanciful, Neely could swear her announcement had halted not only conversation but the rhythmic ticking from the wall clock.

Well, how did you expect them to take it?

Since she'd never actually told her family that she'd been seeing Robert Walsh for the past six months, possibly the last thing they'd expected to hear from Neely was, "I'm getting married."

"To a *man?*" It was Vi who finally spoke. "I mean, you never bring guys home and rarely date, so I always wondered if you were a les—"

"Vidalia Jean!" Mrs. Beth Mason flushed red and actually crossed herself.

Neely rolled her eyes. "Mom, we're not Catholic. And, Vi, I'm not a lesbian."

"Well, congratulations on your engagement," Savannah put in smoothly. "I'm sorry Jason couldn't be here today, he'd want to pass on his felicitations, as well."

"Felicitations?" Vi snorted at their older sister—Savannah beat out Neely by eleven months. "I'm working on a second Master's, and even I don't talk like that. Can't you just say 'Way to go, sis'?"

Douglas, their thirty-nine-year-old brother, stopped eating long enough to tease Vi. "Criticism from someone who had to ask the fiancé's gender?"

Vi shot him a look that was the slightly more mature version of sticking out her tongue, then studied Neely's left hand. "So, where's the rock?"

"We're going to pick it out together."

Robert had proposed last night, on her birthday, giving her two small jewelry boxes after the sumptuous dinner he'd prepared. The first had held a pin, the infinity sign in her birthstone, aquamarine. The second had been empty; he'd told her he'd found his perfect woman, and that if she'd do him the honor of spending the rest of her life with him, they'd find something perfect to fill the ring box. Her lips curved, remembering. He was such a sap, she thought affectionately, not at all who she would have pictured for her husband. Robert was definitely a surprise.

Especially to her family.

Beth cleared her throat, staring pointedly toward her own husband, Gerald Mason, who sat at the head of the table. "Don't you have something to add, dear?"

"Hmm?" The Professor, as everyone called Neely's father, glanced up, his faded blue eyes characteristically preoccupied behind his bifocals.

"For instance," his wife prompted, "asking about who this young man is we've never heard of before today!"

"You've heard of Robert lots of times," Neely said. "I've worked with him for three years, ever since I left the accounting firm and went to work in-house at Becker. I think some of you have even met him."

"Yeah, but that's hardly the same as knowing you're bumping uglies with him."

"Vidalia Jean!"

"What?" Vi looked at their mother, all owl-eyed innocence. "She just turned forty-five. You don't think she's a virgin, do you? Douglas isn't married anymore, but I'll bet no one expects *him* to lead a celibate lifestyle."

"Hey," Douglas protested around a mouthful of potato salad, "my love life isn't the issue today."

Beth could have been a ventriloquist with the way she enunciated her words from behind primly set lips. "Some topics are not appropriate to the dinner table."

"But hearing about Uncle Darnell's colonoscopy last month was okay?" Vi muttered.

Savannah stood, a purposeful smile on her attractive face. "Vi, darlin', why don't you help me clear the table and get candles for Neely's cake? Mama did all the work preparing dinner and it's Neely's celebration, so I think we should be the ones to clean up, don't you?"

Neely was sure the answer to that question would be a resounding no, but Vidalia dutifully scooted her chair back across the gold-and-cream area rug. Then Vi grabbed a couple of dishes from the table, including her brother's plate.

"I was still eating that!"

"Come finish it in the kitchen," his younger sister said tartly. "I've been exiled from the discussion, I don't see why you should get to stay."

As the three of them went into the adjoining room, Douglas explained that if he *had* stayed, Vi would've had a mole who could fill her in later. Neely barely made out Vi's retort that, for a lawyer, Douglas was surprisingly unobservant, only noting "guy things" and skimping on pertinent details.

Neely couldn't decide if she was glad her siblings were gone, or if she felt more nervous facing her parents alone. Well, her mother, anyway, still formidable at sixty-seven. The Professor wasn't the sort who made anyone nervous, unless his history students had feared failing grades back when he taught at the community college.

"You children." Heaving a sigh at her end of the

table, Beth Mason shook her head. Her steel-colored curls, set for the last twenty years at Lana's Beauty Shop, didn't move so much as a strand. "Some people think parenting stops when the kids leave the house, but that's just not so. Take Vidalia for instance—you know the nights I stay up worrying about that girl? And now *you*, who has been nearly as dependable as my Savannah, give us a heart attack with this news that you're getting married out of the blue sky. You're not…in the family way, are you?"

"Pregnant?" Neely choked on a horrified laugh. "At my age?" She had the urge to make the sign of the cross herself.

"I was over forty when I had Vidalia. Turned out to be a good thing, since she would have driven me prematurely gray if I'd had her young. But it's nice to hear you aren't getting married for that reason. I'm glad you're in love. Still, you'd think that would be the sort of thing a girl told her family."

Neely squirmed in her chair. When Robert had kissed her on the beach during an administrative retreat in Key West, she hadn't told anyone—not even her best friend, Leah. What if the incident had been the by-product of fruity green umbrella drinks and nothing more? But shortly after, he'd asked her to come cheer him on at a pool championship and invited her to one of the meet-and-greet cookouts he and several of his apartment neighbors frequently threw. As she and Robert magically passed that invisible barrier between becoming a couple and actual coupledom, she'd shared the news with Leah, but neglected to bring it up during the monthly Sunday dinners with her family. She'd told herself she was forty-five and hardly needed anyone's permission to date, but that wasn't it.

Though her immediate family had finally stopped nagging her about having a man in her life, she knew the second they caught wind of one, the resulting matrimonial pressure would be intense. As would the pressure to have Robert over for dinner. Neely barely made it through these gatherings with her own sanity intact; she was reluctant to subject the man she loved to one.

Of course, she loved her family, too. She just didn't consider them confidantes. Vi was of a completely different generation, Douglas was normally wrapped up in his own life, and Savannah…well, Neely would just as soon keep her Savannah issues repressed. And Lord knew what Robert would make of her parents. He'd thought it was endearingly odd that the Masons had deliberately named all four of their children after Georgia cities, but that wasn't even the tip of her family's idiosyncrasies.

Robert was one of the few people not related by blood who could get away with calling Neely by her given name, Cornelia. The way her mother was glaring at her now, she was about to get the full "Cornelia Annette" treatment.

"I'm sorry, Mom. You know I'm…a private person. At first, I just wasn't comfortable telling you all about him because I wasn't sure where the relationship was going, if anywhere. Then, once a few months had passed, trying to figure out how to backpedal and tell you we were involved was awkward."

"So you waited until the engagement?" Beth arched an eyebrow. "At least we found out before the wedding invitation showed up in the mail. I suppose that's something."

Neely bit back a groan—her mother's sarcasm was partially deserved and entirely expected. It was why she'd asked Robert to let her tell them alone. After she'd accepted his proposal, they'd headed for his bedroom, and she'd floated on bliss and champagne until waking at three in the morning to the realization that she'd have to tell the Masons today. He'd wanted to come with her, but the second her family saw a man walk in, they would have known something was afoot. They would have ferreted out the engagement before she'd even got past the foyer, and everything afterward would have been pointed remarks and interrogation. It seemed an inhospitable way to repay him for such a lovely night.

"How old did you say he was again?" Beth demanded.

I didn't. "Forty-seven."

Her mother sniffed. "Divorced, I suppose."

Neely bit the inside of her lip at her mom's hypocrisy. To her mother, divorced still meant damaged goods and scandal; yet Beth thought her only son could do no wrong, was shocked that his wife had left him and just knew a more deserving woman lurked in his future.

"Actually, Mom, Robert's never been married. We have that in common."

"Pushing fifty and he's never settled down?" Beth narrowed her sharp hazel eyes. "What's wrong with him that no woman would have him? Or is he the kind who runs from commitment?"

"Would you prefer he was divorced?"

"Don't you sass me. I don't care how old you are, I'm still your mama and I won't be sassed at my own table. I'm unhappy enough that this husband-to-be of yours didn't do us the honor of coming to meet us."

"That's my fault. I wanted to tell you alone and stopped him from coming. We argued about it this morning." *Quibbled, anyway.*

Beth looked somewhat mollified. "Well, we should meet him soon."

"As quickly as we can all fit it into our schedules," Neely promised. "I'll call you this week."

"You work with him—is he an accountant, too?"

Which was nicer than the way Vi would have asked. *So is he another soulless number-cruncher?* Neely figured her baby sister had plenty of "soul" for the whole family...maybe not the budget or discipline to pay rent regularly, but definitely spunk and imagination. "Not exactly. He works in market analysis. We collaborate on reports for our boss, especially on prospective deals. Robert's a visionary who puts together projections on the potential benefits of a deal, and I work the figures to make sure it's affordable and evaluate realistic profit margins." They were a good team.

But Beth was interested in different details. "Where are his people from?"

Oh, boy. "His parents live in Lawrenceville."

"So he grew up in Gwinnett?"

"Went to high school there, when they relocated from Vermont. Decades ago." Not that any number of years could help them now, she knew.

"They're *Yankees?*"

That drew signs of life from Gerald Mason.

"During the War Between the States, the Vermont 4th Infantry—"

"Oh, for the love of…" Beth had never, in Neely's memory, actually finished her oft-repeated phrase; the siblings used to make a game of speculating. For the love of God? Probably not, as that would fall under Beth's definition of blasphemy. The love of Mike? Pete? Elvis? Six-armed alien sexbots? The latter being Vi's contribution.

"Gerald, our daughter has informed us that she's taking a husband. Surely you'd like to contribute something to the conversation other than regiment trivia?"

He offered Neely a soft, somehow unfocused smile. If he'd been sitting closer to her, he probably would have patted her on the arm. "Congratulations, sweet pea. Do you need us to pay for the wedding? We certainly have more saved up now than we did when Savannah settled down."

"No, Dad, that's all right." She and Robert might not be rich, but they made decent salaries at Becker Southern Media, and she'd invested wisely. "We've both got savings accounts and can manage a simple affair. We thought June would be—"

"June? That's just three months away," Beth pointed out in a you're-out-of-your-everlovin'-mind tone. People often talked about genteel Southern

Belles, but forgot to mention another traditional figure, the Southern Matriarch, the iron-willed, sharp-eyed woman who usually raised those belles and ran the household. "And what is this folderol about a simple affair? Surely you aren't planning to shame your family."

Neely wondered idly if there were wedding planners who specialized in that—holiday weddings, theme weddings, nuptial events that will make your mama put a paper bag over her head. "I'm planning on getting married, Mother. Shame wasn't part of the equation."

"There's that sass again. You have relatives, Cornelia, people who love you and would be slighted if they didn't get a chance to participate in your big day. We should call Savannah back in here and start making lists immediately. Maybe we should even call Carol and Jo to help! Seems like a month of Sundays since we all got together."

At the mention of her two aunts, a sense of fore-boding rolled through Neely like dark storm clouds through a summer sky. "Mom, Robert and I haven't discussed what kind of wedding—"

"Don't you'd think you'd better hurry if you're going to be married in June? Besides, men don't want to be bothered with things like seating charts and floral ar-rangements! They're grateful for a woman who can handle all of the organizing and just show them where to stand on the big day. Isn't that right, Gerald?"

"Yes, dear."

Neely, however, didn't feel as agreeable. She was familiar enough with Beth's take-charge personality to worry. She didn't want to lose control of her wedding. After all, she'd waited forty-five years to have one, so shouldn't it be the day of her dreams?

Our dreams, she reminded herself guiltily. *Robert's and mine.* She was so used to living her life alone and making plans accordingly.

But all that was about to change.

CHAPTER 2

"You okay, kid?"

Vi sent a glare of female empowerment toward her brother, but the full effect was probably lost behind her tinted sunglasses. "I hate when you call me that."

Douglas gave her a deliberately irritating smirk from the driver's seat. "Why do you think I still do it?"

She laughed despite herself. He had that effect on her—on all women, really. Whether it was making a sister laugh or getting a female client to confide in him, dark-haired, dimpled Douglas was good at charming the ladies. He'd told her it was a shallow talent but not without its uses, especially when it came to jury selection. Or when it had come to sweet-talking their older sisters into covering for him, but that was before her time.

Flipping on his left blinker, he waltzed the luxury sedan across two lanes on 85, toward the exit that led to the run-down duplex Vi shared with a Hispanic single mother and her children. Vi, who used the MARTA bus and subway system as her primary means of getting around, didn't have a car of her own. But that lack was not going to excuse her from monthly Sunday dinners, particularly now that Douglas lived so close.

Geography-wise, anyway.

The condo he'd taken a few blocks from his firm's downtown building seemed worlds away from Vi's weathered brick house with its rusty porch rail and torn window screens; her low-budget rental agreement had stipulated "as is" conditions, making most repairs her responsibility but giving her leniency in terms of redecorating. She kept meaning to spruce up the place, but with classes and three part-time jobs, she had even less time than money. Plus, she wasn't sure how much she wanted to invest when she and another waitress were talking about maybe looking for an apartment together to help lower bills.

"Thanks for the ride home, old man." A fitting response to the *kid* remark. "If I'd had to wait for Savannah, who knows when I would have escaped? They looked like they were settling in for the long haul." June was still a few months off, but their mother had acted as if all the wedding details had to be nailed down today.

"You're not upset they didn't ask you to stay, are you?"

Vi blinked. "For planning all that girlie stuff? Please. I know even less about weddings than you do."

She knew enough about Neely, however, to recognize the trapped expression in her blue eyes as Savannah and Beth tag-teamed her. Savannah could teach Martha Stewart a thing or two about putting together a beautiful event, and Beth, who'd helped raise two younger sisters and then four children of her own, could have organized the entire Confederate Army if she'd been born a century sooner. And if they'd given women meaningful leadership roles. So Vi had no doubts that Neely's wedding would be a lovely, well-run occasion. She just wondered if, between her sister and her mother, any of Neely's personality would show through.

Assuming Neely had one.

Her efficient, detached older sister had a brain like a calculator. Of course, most of Vi's family would say *she* had enough personality for all of them, and they wouldn't mean it as a compliment. The thought bothered her more than it normally would.

With a start, she realized that Neely's announcement today had broken the only real bond she'd shared with her sister. Savannah was perfect and Douglas, if flawed by his divorce, was successful and charming enough to secure his parents' adoration. But Neely's "spinsterhood" had always earned their mother's and aunts' disapproval, much like Vi's…everything.

"Well, here we are." Douglas pulled onto the cracked driveway that led up to the left half of the double-home. On the parallel right-hand strip of pavement, a shirtless teenager had his head stuck under the hood of an old blue Cadillac. Douglas flicked his gaze in that direction. "You may not have a car for me to work on, but I've been meaning to ask, do you, um, need a little help with repairs on this place?"

Since she doubted her brother had lifted a hammer his entire adult life, she snorted at the offer. "Mom said something to you about my disgraceful living conditions."

"While also managing to cast aspersions on my manhood and ability with power tools."

The idea of Douglas near a power tool made Vi's fingers itch to dial 911. Zoe, his ex, used to joke that he drank straight Scotch over ice because he couldn't even build a decent drink. Vi had liked the woman and occasionally still ran into her on campus, where the willowy brunette taught a civics class. At thirty-seven the former Mrs. Mason was attractive enough that Vi wouldn't be surprised if freshman boys had hot-for-teacher fantasies over her.

For that matter, Vi had reason to believe her brother still fantasized about Zoe on a regular basis. Their divorce was no healthier than their marriage had been, but given Vi's own dysfunctional love life, she wasn't one to judge. Her relationships seemed to come in two modes—low-key fun with guys she knew she'd never stay with long, and passionate flings characterized by intense sex but too much fighting. Frankly, until today's revelation, she'd always wondered if Neely had the right idea by staying single.

Oblivious to Vi's mental meandering, Douglas was still defending his masculinity. "All right, so I'm not…some guy famous for renovating stuff. My employers must not think I'm useless because they pay me pretty damn well. Even if I don't rescreen your windows myself, I can certainly write you a check to get it done."

Yes he could, without even blinking. It was so Douglas to offer the easy solution.

She sighed, wishing his attempted generosity didn't leave her feeling snide. "Nah, I'd probably just blow the money on booze and extreme makeovers." Besides, if she really needed something fixed, she could always ask Brendan, her most recent low-key boyfriend, a nice guy with whom she had little in common.

As if she were the kid he'd jokingly called her,

Douglas reached over and tousled her hair, a chin-length platinum shag. "I like this, but I kept waiting for Mom to say something about it."

Please. As if Savannah hadn't been dyeing her hair for years? Or did Douglas think it was *naturally* retaining its youthful gold, unmarred by the hereditary gray that streaked Neely's ash-blond bob? Vi had heard their mother sigh to Neely as they'd set out the china, "I suppose that awful bleaching is better than some of the colors Vidalia could have chosen."

She forced a laugh. "Pointless to say something about it now that it's done, isn't it? Besides, I'm a grown-up, and it's my hair."

Douglas stared at her for a long, unsmiling second, then ducked his head, a wry grin and one dimple evident in profile. "You're no more a responsible grown-up than I am. We just play different games, is all."

Savannah parked The Tank, her SUV, wondering if she'd ever be completely comfortable maneuvering the vehicle into her half of the garage. When Trent left for university next fall and she was officially beyond her toting-children-around years, maybe she'd buy something small and sleek. The thought should have made her smile, but instead a cold shadow passed through her. It seemed like only yesterday her sons had been strapped into car seats behind her, pelting each other with Cheerios.

She unfastened her seat belt with a sigh, her mood not lightened by the realization that she should have called. Arriving home late with no word was the kind of behavior that would have earned her boys a reprimand. Even though her husband and youngest son knew she'd been with her family, a lot could have happened between Kennesaw and Roswell. She'd been so caught up in the excitement of Neely's wedding plans that she'd forgotten to phone them so they didn't worry and let them know what dinner options were in the refrigerator.

But a voice that sounded more like one of her sisters' than hers whispered, *Trent is seventeen and Jason has a medical degree, they can darn well open the fridge and see for themselves what's available.* Okay, maybe that didn't sound exactly like her sisters. She couldn't imagine no-nonsense Neely saying *darn,* and the thought of Vi using such a watered-down expression was enough to restore Savannah's grin as she opened the door that led into her spacious navy-and-white kitchen. Sunflower accents added bright splashes of cheer.

Although she hadn't done any baking today, the room smelled as homey and delicious as it did on

Thanksgiving, thanks to the cinnamon spice pot-pourri she kept in the windowsill over the double sink. She worked hard to make this house a comfortable, inviting place to live. Whether he was capable of checking in the refrigerator or not wasn't the point—Jason Carter, one of Atlanta's best obstetricians, worked long, draining shifts and provided well for his wife and two sons. The least *she* could do was insure he came home to lovingly prepared meals and clean rooms.

The kitchen was unsurprisingly empty. Though the women in her family were known for congregating in kitchens, Savannah's sons and husband normally gravitated toward the big-screen television. She heard muffled sounds from the den down the hallway.

"I'm home," she called out, kicking off her shoes before she padded across the pale carpeting.

Trent and Jason were both in the den, her son stretched across the couch with his size twelve sneakers on the velour arm, and her husband sprawled in the recliner she'd bought him for Christmas. An open cardboard box on the coffee table between them revealed two uneaten slices of pizza, and while both men said hello, neither looked away from the basketball game they were watching.

"Honestly, Trent, you're old enough to know

better than to put your shoes on my furniture." And a shower after his softball practice wouldn't have killed him, either.

"Sorry." He bent toward his feet with teenage flexibility, tossing the shoes to the ground with muffled thuds while his gaze stayed locked on the foul shot being made. Now the room smelled like sweat socks and sausage pizza—she squelched the urge to run for her vacuum cleaner and some carpet deodorizer.

"I hope you two weren't worried about me," she said, feeling like an idiot even as the words left her mouth. The glassy-eyed, sauce-smeared faces before her did not hold expressions of concern. "I know I'm normally back long before dinnertime, but—"

"Now that you mention it." Trent craned his head, his hazel eyes finally meeting hers as he flashed her an impish grin. "What are we having?"

It was just plain sad that some part of her was pleased by his request, felt gratifyingly needed. "Didn't you have pizza already?"

He crinkled his nose. "That was an afternoon snack. I'm starved. But I can finish off those last two slices if you don't want to cook, Mom."

"I don't mind." The words came out too fast, the echo of desperation worse than the locker-room-meets-pizzeria aroma. "Any special requests, Jason?"

Her husband shook his head. "I made the mistake of having a piece of our son's killer pizza when I got in and have the heartburn to show for it. I'll probably take some antacid and hit the sack early."

"Deliveries go okay?" she asked.

"One emergency C, but all mothers and babies are in good health. I'm exhausted, though. I swear I could just sleep here—this chair's even more comfortable than our bed."

If Trent hadn't been in the room, would she have flirted a little, teased that she'd miss her husband if he didn't come to bed? The truth was, with the crazy hours he sometimes worked, she was accustomed to sleeping alone. Besides, his snoring on the mattress next to her didn't always make her feel less lonely.

She forced a bright smile, not that anyone was looking at her. "Well, I have big news! You'll never believe who's getting married—Neely."

That got their attention. Jason looked up, grunting in surprise. "Neely? I half expected you to say Vi followed a wild impulse and ran off with her pottery instructor or something."

"Aunt Cornelia?" Trent's mouth had fallen open. "Wow. Why?"

Men. "Because she's in love."

Her son ran a hand through his dark hair, considering. "I guess. It's just weird to think about someone her age, you know, dating."

"She's younger than I am."

"Sure, but not by much and you're a mom. You've got grown kids. You don't date!"

No, she didn't. She went with her son to scout universities and planned meals, making jokes about how much her grocery bill would drop once she no longer had teenage boys in the house. Reverting to type now, she left the guys to their game and retreated to the kitchen, deciding a chef salad would work nicely for her and Trent's dinner. It had been tough when Adam, her twenty-year-old, left for school, but having Trent at home had helped ease the ache. Once he was gone, her life would be so…

Quiet. She tried to put a relaxing spin on the word. Less stressful without a seventeen-year-old and his appalling musical taste. She wouldn't have to wait up on Saturday nights, lying in bed and listening for him to come home from his dates. Oh, who did she think she was kidding? With her baby out on his own, she'd probably lie in bed worrying about him *every* night. Hoping he didn't fall in with the wrong kids, wondering if he was keeping on top of his course work, praying he didn't get some pretty young coed pregnant.

Jason had chuckled at those same concerns when

Adam left for university. "You raised good kids," her husband had assured her. "Now it's time to let them go and become the men they'll be."

Raised good kids—past tense. She'd been a full-time mom and housewife for two decades. Her days were going to be strangely empty without PTA meetings, doctors' appointments, football booster club. Not that she felt sorry for herself. She was proud of her nearly grown sons, and aware of her blessings. How many of her friends and neighbors had marveled over Savannah's life?

You're so together, Savannah, I could never be that organized!

You have such great boys.

How on earth do you find time to cook like this—and with such sinful desserts, how do you stay so trim?

She knew she was lucky.

It was just...since she didn't turn forty-six until late April, Savannah and her sister were the same age one month out of every year. She and Neely were both forty-five. So, why did it seem like Neely's life was about to hit a new beginning while Savannah's, in so many ways, seemed to be coming to a close?

"So, how'd it go?" Because Robert was too kind to hold grudges, there was no lingering annoyance in his gray eyes, no resentment that Neely had argued against his coming to lunch. There was only affection and a hint of amusement.

"Great." She leaned against his kitchen counter, where breakfast and lunch dishes were stacked. Must not have been room for them in the sink—not with last night's dinner plates, abandoned in passionate haste, still piled beneath the faucet. "It went great."

Other than Vi thinking she was a lesbian, her divorced brother becoming uncharacteristically withdrawn after he'd absorbed the wedding news and their mother's insistence on calling Neely's soon-to-be in-laws the *Yankees*.

With a sigh, she abandoned the pretense. "My family makes me crazy."

Robert laughed. "Isn't that what families are for, to offset all the needless sanity in our lives?"

Grinning back at him felt good. "Then my mother deserves some kind of award for going above and beyond. She's known about the wedding less than twelve hours, and already she's trying to take over. How many groomsmen were you thinking, because she's suggesting distant cousins I swear I've never met to be bridesmaids."

"Groomsmen? Well, there's Stuart, of course. Maybe Bryan. Is it okay that I haven't actually given this part much thought? I've only been engaged for a day."

Engaged. Her heart fluttered at the newness of it, the wonder that she'd found someone who wanted to spend his life with her. "Of course it's okay that we haven't figured out the details yet. One step at a time. But it might have simplified my life, at least short term, if I'd waited until later to tell her."

His arms fell to her waist, and he pulled her closer. "How much later?"

"Umm…June?"

He chuckled again, as he so often did. Robert had a perfect laugh, deep and warm—neither self-conscious titters, nor the loud, my-jokes-are-so-funny bray of a guy who pokes fun at others. Merely the comfortable reaction of a man who saw the humor in life. And helped her see it more clearly.

She'd always been reserved, figuring someone in the family should be. She wasn't like outgoing Savannah who knew the perfect response to every social occasion, mouthy Vi who delighted in audaciousness, or Douglas, who, in the course of charming and joking his way through life, sometimes failed to respect the gravity of a situation. Except for one disastrous period of college rebellion she didn't like to remember, Neely had clung to hard work and staying focused. As a result, she now held a good position working for Cameron Becker. Seriousness had served her well.

It just hadn't gotten her laid very often, Vi would point out.

Neely's relationships with men who matched her personality had been sensible, but boring. On the other hand, her two affairs with guys her polar opposite had ended badly, the first in college which had left her humiliated and heartbroken, the second just before she hit forty. She'd ended the latter relationship quickly, before she killed the man and had to retain Douglas to defend her.

But now she had Robert. It was one of life's ironies that she'd found her perfect balance when she wasn't even looking. Between all the time she'd devoted to work and the girls' nights she'd spent helping Leah through her separation and eventual divorce, Neely had barely dated in four years before Robert kissed her on that beach.

She snuggled into his shoulder, the memory of sea air superimposed over the familiar smell of his aftershave. "If the end result is marrying you, I can handle anything my mother dishes out over the next three months."

"I love you, too."

"Just remember that later this week, okay?" Neely finally had escaped her parents' house today with sworn oaths to bring Robert over in a few days and discuss wedding plans more then. The thought of the coming conversations made her head hurt. "You're sure I can't talk you into eloping?" Quick, simple, and no worries about assigning someone to keep cousin Phoebe away from the bar.

"Sorry." He grinned that rakish smile that made his eyes crinkle at the corners. "Since I've waited so long to find the right bride, I insist we do the wedding right. Have you recruited Leah as your maid of honor yet? Maybe she can help run interference with your mom."

Recalling the shadowed expression in Douglas's eyes before he'd left, Neely struggled against a wince. It was tough to share the news of your engagement with someone whose own marriage had collapsed. Still, she knew Leah would be thrilled for her. It should help that her friend already knew about Robert and that she'd been divorced considerably longer than Neely's brother.

"I'm telling her tomorrow. I asked her this morning if we could meet for lunch."

"Well, then. That will take care of the most important people, except…"

"Your parents." She'd never met them, but since they were the people who'd raised Robert, she assumed they were wonderful.

"They'll be back from their cruise by next weekend. Not nervous, are you?"

"No." Sure, she'd experienced the odd apprehensive moment over informing the future in-laws that their only child was taking a bride, but it had to be easier than dealing with her family today. "Your family's normal, right?"

He grinned. "*Normal* is such a relative term."

CHAPTER 3

Neely strode through the Lenox Square Mall, which was pretty crowded for a Monday. Leah worked as a cosmetics consultant in one of the upscale department stores, so they were meeting in one of the restaurants inside the mall. Declining a sample of teriyaki chicken as she passed the food court and zigzagging around two women oohing and ahhing over some Kenneth Cole shoes outside a store window, Neely recalled how Leah had sounded on the phone yesterday morning. Distracted, sniffly. Her friend had claimed seasonal allergies and the disorienting effects of antihistamine, which was certainly plausible in Georgia this time of year. If it had been twelve months ago, or even six, Neely would have assumed that Leah was crying over her rat bastard ex-husband, but her friend seemed adjusted to her single life lately.

She looks terrific, anyway. Neely watched Leah step

off the escalator. With her wave of red-gold hair and slimming uniform of black turtleneck and slacks, she was easy to spot among browsing housewives in pastel spring fashions. Whereas Neely had put on a few pounds after lingering over meals with Robert, Leah had lost at least fifteen since her divorce, largely because she took out her aggression in workouts at a women's gym. Her body was in the best shape it had been since Neely had known her.

But as the two women came to a stop within a few feet of each other beneath the emerald awning of the agreed-upon bar and grill, Neely could see Leah's pretty face sported more makeup than usual. Still not enough to disguise her red and slightly swollen eyes.

Antihistamines, my ass. "You've been crying." At times like this, she wished she had Savannah's diplomatic knack of knowing what to say.

"Not in the last five minutes," Leah said, trying to make a joke of it with her wobbly smile.

"Well, let's get you to a table, I'll buy you lunch and you can tell me what's wrong."

"Okay, but I don't actually have much of an appetite and margaritas are a no-no since I have to go back to work right after this. Don't want unsteady hands while I'm wielding a mascara wand near a customer's eye."

An impossibly skinny hostess with towering heels and a fall of straight, glossy hair showed them to a booth. Neely hoped for the pretty young woman's sake that she had someone to rub her feet at the end of her shift—standing all day in those shoes couldn't be comfortable.

Even though Leah had said she wasn't hungry and Neely's blood pressure didn't need the salt, they ordered tortilla chips with the restaurant's signature spinach dip. Placing drink orders and waiting for the appetizer to come gave Leah a little time to regain her composure.

Once her friend looked less fragile, Neely hazarded a guess. "Did something happen with Phillip to upset you?"

"You could say that." Leah's soft brown eyes brimmed with tears.

"We don't *have* to talk about it, I just—"

"No, you'll find out soon enough anyway. I imagine news will work itself through the office."

Phillip was an employee of Becker Southern Media. Neely didn't work closely with him, but had come to know Leah through accumulated company picnics, Christmas parties and other social gatherings.

"He's getting married," Leah blurted. "He called me Saturday afternoon, oozing his newfound happiness. He said he wanted to tell me because he didn't want me to find out accidentally from you or another mutual acquaintance. A plausible excuse, but I can't help

thinking he wanted to gloat a little. The worst part…"
A sob welled up, choking off the rest of her sentence.

Neely snapped a chip in half, imagining it was Phillip's neck.

"The worst part is, it's not Kate."

Six years younger and two cup sizes larger than Leah, Kate was the woman Phillip had been sleeping with when his wife dissolved the marriage.

"You wish it *was?*"

"I keep thinking I'd feel better if he'd ended up with her, if he'd cheated on me because he really loved her. Knowing that he threw our marriage away over a meaningless fling… He proposed to Tiffany, a more recent girlfriend and even younger than Kate. Not quite half his age, but close enough. Tiffany and Phillip? Why doesn't he just send out wedding announcements that say 'You're invited to my midlife crisis'? He told me he'd be honored if I can come to the ceremony, but that he would understand if it was *too painful*." She sneered the last words in a parody of concern.

"Bastard," Neely muttered. "Serve him right if you showed up looking hot as all hell, with a twenty-five-year-old stud on your arm."

Leah managed a smile. "That idea has merit. Or would, if I knew any twenty-five-year-old studs who wouldn't call me ma'am."

"This is Georgia, women of all ages get called ma'am."

"Still. I don't really want to go to the wedding, except that I'm sure if I don't, he'll assume it's because I'm not over his sorry ass."

Are you?

Reading the unasked question in Neely's expression, Leah continued. "I thought I was, but this wedding news hit me hard. I mean, I got weepy this morning when a woman bought an assortment of lipsticks and told me they were party favors for a bridal shower. Am I pathetic enough to still be in love with a man who thought to have and to hold meant just until something curvier sauntered along?"

"You're not pathetic! He sandbagged you with this announcement, and you're having a normal reaction. Whether you go or not, what he thinks doesn't matter." And if there was justice in the world, he'd be struck impotent on his wedding night.

"Well, I have plenty of time to decide." Leah fiddled with the straw in her soft drink. "They haven't even set a date yet. Not that I needed to know this, apparently little Tiffany has always dreamed of a June wedding, but says this summer doesn't give her enough time to plan and next summer is much too far away for her to wait. A June wedding—how cliché is that?"

Neely swallowed. More of a gulp actually. She'd

been so incensed on her friend's behalf that she'd temporarily forgotten why she'd asked Leah to meet her for lunch in the first place. *Well*, now's *hardly the time to tell her*.

But she'd have to tell Leah eventually, and her friend would want details—when, where and how Robert had proposed. Once she found out, she'd be hurt Neely hadn't told her immediately. "Uh…Leah? You might know someone else guilty of that same cliché."

"What, you mean getting married in June? Who?"

Raising her hand level with her face, she said tentatively, "Me."

"Huh? *Oh, my God!* Robert proposed?"

"Yeah. We can wait until later to talk about it, but you're my best friend. It wouldn't be right if you weren't one of the first people to know."

"Of course we have to talk about it! I don't want you to think…oh, dear. You're getting married in June? Sorry about the crack earlier. You understand that *you* are a classy woman who appreciates tradition, while Tiffany is an airhead who doesn't have an original thought."

"Ooh, nice distinction."

Dashing away tears—happier ones this time—Leah glanced around. "Where is our waitress? A discussion like this should take place over a celebratory lunch and decadent desserts."

But at the office a couple of hours later, dessert was churning in Neely's stomach.

Was it warm in the conference room, or was she the only one who felt overheated and slightly nauseous? It occurred to her she might be having a hot flash—and wouldn't *that* be sexy with her fiancé sitting directly across from her?—but even though her doctor had confirmed she was definitely perimenopausal, she suspected this was a result of lunch.

She tried to concentrate on the current discussion about an upcoming radio merger, but her conversation with Leah kept intruding. For all of her friend's determination to be happy for her, Neely had still left lunch feeling overwhelmed. Leah's hyperenthusiastic questions had been the equal but opposite reaction to Beth Mason's caustic remarks and forceful suggestions. Leah had cheerfully reeled off inquiry after inquiry, each landing like lead on top of the fudge sundae they'd shared.

"Will it be a church wedding?"

"I don't know. I'd always had in the back of my mind that a garden wedding would be nice, but Mom pointed out that Aunt Jo is allergic to practically everything and that you can never guarantee the weather."

"Well, you'll want to reserve a venue immediately!

Places book early for June. Speaking of places, are you moving into his?"

"I don't know." It shocked Neely that she hadn't even considered that yet. She was a details person, the one who usually worried about logistics. Still, she'd been swept up in the novelty of romance, being in love and enjoying that for once in her life. Besides, she had months left on her lease and time to discuss the situation with Robert.

"So, will the two of you be getting a prenup? If I had *my* farce of a marriage to do all over again, I certainly would—not that you and Robert will ever need one!"

But who ever really thought they'd need a prenup? How could Leah have guessed, the day she optimistically took her vows, that she'd now be debating whether or not to attend her husband's second wedding? Certainly Douglas had seemed shell-shocked, despite warnings, when Zoe followed through on her threat to leave if he couldn't grow up and take more responsibility in their relationship.

Neely had never even been engaged, let alone married, but she remembered the mocking disregard with which her first lover had cast her aside, leaving her dumbfounded and gun-shy. She knew now that she hadn't loved him, had merely been infatuated and pleased to have someone's full attention after years of living with a perfect sister and the brother who would carry on the family name. If being unceremoniously dumped had crushed her then, how much pain would it cause if *Robert* ever decided to leave? She imagined the last thing she'd want to deal with under those circumstances would be tangled divorce settlements that only prolonged goodbye.

"Neely?" Cameron Becker's gruff voice penetrated her thoughts, and she jumped guiltily in the padded office chair. "You're scowling. You don't agree with Dave's assessment?"

From farther down the table, vice president David Samuels frowned at her.

Oops. "No, I think he was…dead-on. I'm sorry, just got distracted for a moment. Is it hot in here?"

Amanda Barnes, a fifty-something consultant working with Becker on this deal, shot her a sympathetic glance. Robert looked concerned and followed her to her office after the meeting.

"Feeling okay?" he asked once they were alone.

"I guess lunch didn't agree with me." She sipped the cup of water she'd poured in the hall.

He sat on the corner of her desk, a little close for her comfort to an expenditure report she'd typed that morning. "You mean just the food, right? Or was telling Leah really that bad?"

"No, she—hang on, why don't we move this out of the way?" She'd been known to use binder clips that coordinated with the colors of her fonts and graphs; she was not handing Cameron a crinkled report. "She was very happy for us. But the timing stank. Turns out Phillip just informed her he was getting remarried."

"Ouch."

Neely crossed the room to refile some of the folders she'd needed earlier. "She was great, though. Very excited about being the maid of honor. I know I said yesterday that we have time to think about the details, but Leah made a good point. We should reserve a place immediately. If not sooner. So we might want to think about what size crowd we're looking at, whether we want a formal dinner or more casual reception."

He nodded affably, looking utterly relaxed in the face of her rising panic. This was why he was so good for her. "Why don't you come over, I'll grab takeout on the way home, and we can start planning?"

"Or we could go to my place," she threw out impulsively. Maybe it was territorial of her, but she couldn't relax as well at Robert's place. And not just because of the constant drop-ins of neighbors who were fond of her extroverted fiancé, including Sheila, the thirty-eight-year-old downstairs he had once dated. They'd never become very serious, but she continued to depend on Robert's help with her car and occasional handyman jobs if it was the weekend and the super was out of touch. It was amazing how many maintenance issues Sheila had over the weekend.

Neighbors aside, Neely always had the urge to tidy Robert's apartment. Her birthday had been a notable exception since he'd gone to great pains to clean up and set a romantic atmosphere in the main rooms. For his cluttered guest room, he'd shut the door and left it at that.

His eyebrows lifted, but after a moment, he said, "Sure. Either way."

"Sorry. I think…maybe because I'm not feeling well, I'm sort of longing for the comforts of home."

"Understood." He slid off the desk and came toward her, as if about to offer a hug, but stopped shy. Although it was common knowledge they were a couple, they'd agreed early on to keep displays of affection away from the workplace. "I'll meet you there at about seven?"

"Sounds great, thank you." The man was a gem.

Pausing at the door, he asked, "You don't feel uncomfortable at my place, do you? I hope you know you can make yourself at home there. I can clear some closet space for you, give you some drawers in the bathroom. Anything that helps."

"That's sweet, but not necessary. Your place is already very homey." It definitely had that lived-in feel.

After he'd gone, she sat behind her desk, pondering the questions Leah had posed. Did Robert think they'd move into his place? Hers was closer to the office, but not as big. Then again, he didn't exactly make the most of the space he had. She wouldn't call his apartment grungy, but it *was* the home of a mellow bachelor who got around to sorting his laundry when he felt like it. He just fished clean socks out of the laundry basket on the sofa as needed.

Neely tackled household chores with a practical the-sooner-the-better approach. They'd had more than one dinner at her place where Robert had invited her to sit on the couch and watch television with him and worry about the dishes later; except she was best able to enjoy what she was doing when she knew there wasn't housework waiting afterward. He'd probably understand that about her more once they were living together.

Her temperature spiked again, and her heart thundered in her ears. *We're going to be living together.* She'd known it rationally, she just hadn't stopped to think about it yet. To *really* think about all that it entailed. She'd been on her own for a long time. Even when she did spend a night at Robert's, she knew she could return to her apartment. After June, there would be no "her place" or "his place."

Only the home of Mr. and Mrs. Robert Walsh.

They obviously had a lot more to talk about than how many invitations they should buy and the size of the wedding party. Her stomach tightened at the thought of how many important and personal conversations they needed to have. Her lack of romantic experience left her feeling unprepared, and the uncertainty reminded her why she liked numbers so much. Calculating equations was a lot simpler than being in love. Good thing she'd somehow managed to find a man so worth the trouble—now she just had to prove that she was.

Savannah didn't know why *she* felt so nervous—she was neither the one getting married, nor the stranger coming to meet the family for the first time. Nonetheless, when she handed her mama the sweet potato casserole she'd brought, her fingers were trembling.

Hoping her mother and husband hadn't noticed, she turned to Jason. "Want me to hang up your coat, honey?" Even though it had been warm a few days earlier, the March wind had blown in a storm front that was causing lower temperatures and sinus headaches all over the metroplex.

"Thanks." Her husband held out his jacket and turned to face Douglas, who stood to the side in the parlor with Vi and their father. "So, when do we get to meet the new guy?"

"Neely called to say they got hung up in traffic but should be here in about ten minutes. Can I fix you a drink?" He indicated the side bar, where the Professor was refilling his own glass.

Jason shook his head. "No, thank you. I'm not technically scheduled to work tonight, but I'm on call as backup."

A tug of premature disappointment pulled at Savannah. Jason had missed the last two monthly dinners and been called away from her father's birthday celebration because of work. She hoped that wouldn't be the case tonight—she felt bad enough that Trent couldn't come because of a senior prom fund-raiser. Then again, interruptions were bound to occur when you were married to the man hundreds of women wanted to deliver their babies.

As she put his coat in the entryway closet, Savannah remembered how proud she'd been when she'd told acquaintances she was marrying a doctor! Not that he'd been a doctor at the time, but he'd already been accepted into med school and his path was clear. They'd married after graduating college, and she'd taught at a private day care, helping to shoulder the bills while he studied and interned.

When she'd discovered she was pregnant with Adam, she'd been first ecstatic, then worried about her husband's reaction. They'd planned to wait another year or two before having a baby, but Jason had been thrilled. She'd teased him at prenatal checkups when he'd shown as much interest in the medical equipment as her progress, and she'd wept watching him cradle their son for the first time. If Jason hadn't cried, his eyes had certainly been damp with emotion.

Recalling that moment in the hospital as if it were yesterday, she suddenly felt more generously disposed to the expecting women who so frequently needed Jason's time. After all, when he couldn't make family plans, it was because he was away, bringing the miracle of new life into the world, not because he was waving one-dollar bills in the air at some smoke-filled strip club on the seedier side of Atlanta. She'd known the specifics of being a doctor's wife—odd hours, being a good hostess when he invited members of the medical community for dinner, attending different social functions. Jason had praised her on many occasions for making him look good, saying he'd be lost without her.

Her mood bolstered, Savannah went to help her

mother in the kitchen. It was a sure bet Vi wouldn't think to offer *her* assistance.

Beth had just started to carve the ham when the doorbell pealed through the old house.

"Looks as if our guests of honor are here." Savannah had a sudden moment of reverse déjà vu that caused her smile to falter—would Adam be bringing home a woman to meet his parents in the next few years?

"Late," Beth grunted, looking at the digital over the oven.

Savannah could tell this was another strike against the mysterious suitor who hadn't bothered to meet Neely's parents, much less ask their permission, before proposing. "I'm sure the delay was unavoidable, Mama, and not a reflection on Mr. Walsh."

Her mother slanted her a knowing glance. "You're not about to remind me to be hospitable in my own house, are you?"

"When you're the one who taught me everything *I* know about Southern generosity? Of course not," Savannah said sweetly. "You'd be the perfect gracious hostess to anyone who came to your door, even if they weren't entirely punctual."

Beth grinned. "With some coaching from you, Vidalia could be a lot more subtle about her back talk."

Savannah thought of her sister, of her bright

bleached hair and constant opinions. "I don't think Vi has any interest in subtle."

"Well, let's go join them before she says something to scare off this Robert Walsh and Cornelia ends up as alone and crazy as my great-aunt Willa."

Either Robert and Neely hadn't bothered with jackets, or someone had already put them away. The two of them sat on the striped antique settee Gerald had reupholstered when Savannah was in high school—Neely in a scoop-necked sweater and black skirt, Robert in a button-down shirt and navy tie. He was handsome, Savannah thought judiciously, taking in the wave of silver in his rich brown hair and the sparkle of his gray eyes. The sparkle increased when he looked at Neely, which he did often. She didn't seem to mind, snuggling close to him with her hand resting atop his knee. A simple touch, but meaningful for Neely.

Robert Walsh wasn't quite debonair, but something more comfortable and sincere. Though he was tall, with a firm, square jaw, there was a kind of indefinable softness about him, too. Perhaps Savannah recognized it because it reminded her vaguely of her father, an invisible vibe of kindness that promised he'd never mistreat children or small animals.

When Neely glanced up at her, Savannah's first

instinct was to turn away and not be caught staring. Silly, really, since it was understandable for the family to be curious about Robert. She stepped forward, offering her hand.

"Savannah Mason Carter," she introduced herself. "Have you already met my husband, Dr. Jason Carter?"

"We were just starting the name exchange," Douglas said. "We'd only gotten as far as Dad and Vidalia Jean."

"Who goes by Vi, right?" Robert smiled, looking as if he might say more, perhaps about how Neely didn't like her full name, either, but stopped, catching sight of Beth behind Savannah. Apparently he had the good sense not to joke about names when the people who'd picked them out were standing in the room. "Mrs. Mason. It's a pleasure to finally meet you."

As he held out the bottle of wine he'd brought along as a hostess gift, Savannah grinned inwardly. She liked the "finally" as a discreet reminder that, if it had been up to him, he'd have met them sooner. Robert Walsh might just hold his own with Beth, and once she approved of him, he was family.

After the pleasantries were exchanged, Beth planted her hands on her ample hips. "Well, not to discount the value of small talk, but I worked too hard on that food to let it go cold. Why don't we move into the dining room?"

They all headed that way, and Savannah noticed the hand Robert placed on the small of her sister's back. An odd ripple of yearning went through her at the unconscious intimacy conveyed in the touch. She cast a glance toward her husband, abashedly aware of the longing that probably showed in her face.

But he was deep in discussion with Douglas about a new property tax and didn't notice.

CHAPTER 4

Well, he can't say I didn't warn him, Neely thought.

Robert had assured her before they arrived that he was marrying *her*, so nothing her family said or did would affect his decision. She was holding him to that. Not that her family was being unwelcoming. Far from it—they'd expressed great gratitude that someone had finally proposed to her, and they were trying to make Robert's life easier by mapping out his wedding for him.

"You could always get married here," Gerald volunteered. "This old house might need a bit of spit-shine to polish her up, but she's a historic beauty."

"That she is," Beth agreed, "but too small to properly host their wedding. I imagine you'll have one hundred and fifty guests at least."

"What?" Neely's head reeled. When she and Robert had started discussing wedding specifics Monday night, they'd predicted around seventy-five people, one hundred as the absolute maximum. "I think you're shooting a little high, Mom."

"Nonsense. Savannah and I started a list after you left the other day. That was our conservative estimate, since you insisted on something 'simple.'"

Neely shot her older sister an accusing glance, but it crashed and broke on the shore of Savannah's good intentions.

"No need to thank me!" Savannah said cheerfully. "I want to help in any way possible. Jason and I were so young when we got married that we couldn't really plan a grand affair, and I hardly think at my age I'm going to have a daughter. So planning your wedding will be fun!"

A thrill a minute. Neely wasn't sure how she felt about the unspoken comparison to the daughter Savannah would never have. *I'm only younger by eleven months!* Yet she supposed she'd be getting Savannah's "big sister" treatment for the rest of her life. After all, look at the bossy way Beth still treated her sisters, Carol and Josephine, continuing to this day to issue for-your-own-good orders.

Then again, that was pretty much the way Neely's mom treated *everyone*.

"I think a church wedding would be lovely," Beth

said now, her latest command masquerading as an opinion. "Robert, you're not Catholic, by any chance? Cornelia is a staunch Methodist, so I'm afraid a wedding Mass is out of the question."

"We were going to be staunch Southern Baptists," Vi said to no one in particular, "until we found out they frown on drinking. Although maybe a Baptist wedding gets you out of the obligatory dancing at the reception?"

Her mother shot her the glare of doom, then turned back just in time to hear Robert explain that his parents were Episcopalian.

Their denomination wasn't a big issue for Neely. She prayed and managed to get to church at least once a season, but felt hypocritical describing herself as a "staunch" anything. She also thought that if any kind of ceremony was out of the question, she should be the one making that call, not her mother. But Robert, bless him, took all of Beth's suggestions and Vi's colorful commentary in stride.

The brief panic Neely had experienced in her office earlier this week had receded. Two people making one life together would be complex, but Robert was definitely the man for her. She hadn't been given a choice when it came to her family, but Robert was actually opting to align himself with the Masons instead of fleeing in the other direction. That took courage and character.

"So, you have any siblings?" Douglas asked. "Brothers or, God help you, sisters?"

Robert grinned. "Neither. Just me and my parents. My dad has a brother back in Vermont—are you okay, Mrs. Mason?"

"Fine, fine."

Neely could see how the harrumph her mother made whenever a place north of the Mason-Dixon was mentioned *could* sound as though the woman was choking.

"I have a handful of relatives left there," Robert said. "We're not a big family."

"And the two of you don't plan to make it any bigger by having more little Walshes?" Beth asked.

"Uh—" Robert shot Neely his first truly alarmed look of the evening.

She knew how he felt. Her accountant's brain was already spinning. Even if they hurried and had a baby in the next two years—which they would probably have to do, if she actually wanted to get pregnant before menopause—she would still be in her sixties before the kid could get a driver's license.

"Cornelia Mason Walsh," Douglas said absently, changing the subject. Maybe he'd learned some tact from his courtroom experiences, after all. "That'll take some getting used to. Are you hyphenating, ditching the maiden name altogether or staying as is?"

"What do you mean, *as is?*" Gerald asked, his expression genuinely befuddled. "She won't be *as is,* she'll be a married lady."

"Not all women change their last names," Vi said. "It's the new millennium, Dad. Why should a woman give up her identity just because of an archaic ceremony? I was reading an article about how some modern couples legalize a completely new married name by combining syllables of their separate last names. You guys could be Mr. and Mrs. Walson."

Savannah blinked. "That's in*sane.*"

A scathing denouncement coming from Savannah, Neely thought. Watching her two sisters debate could be interesting, but Beth was already steering the topic to ceremony specifics.

"If Robert comes from a small family and isn't planning on many groomsmen, maybe we should scale back the number of bridesmaids attending Cornelia."

"Scale back?" Neely echoed. "From what? I never decided on a number."

"Three's good," her mother pronounced. "Obviously, you'll want your two sisters and that friend of yours—Lee?"

"Leah. I asked her to be my maid of honor this morning."

From there, suggestions seemed to fly at her randomly—Vi's dictates on what she would or most certainly *would not* be willing to wear at the wedding, Savannah's advice on a caterer she'd just read about in a local magazine and even Jason, mentioning a remote getaway one of his fellow practitioners had vacationed at, in case they were looking for honeymoon ideas.

Neely was overwhelmed by the "help." She'd had a long time to grow accustomed to keeping her own counsel. While she normally sought Robert's and Leah's opinion on important matters, that was far different than half a dozen people all having ideas on what she should do. Granted, Beth always had an opinion, but until recently, Neely had been able to minimize exposure to her mom to once a month. Now, she felt as if she could barely keep up with the conversation aimed at her.

Robert's hand found hers under the table, and she sighed, releasing some of the tension in her body. As overwhelming as the evening might be, she didn't have to deal with it alone. Funny how comforting that thought was for someone so self-sufficient.

We're living in a world gone mad. That was Vi's conclusion as everyone adjourned to the parlor after dessert. Beth was still issuing matrimonial orders like a wedding planner on steroids, between asking

Savannah to help with the coffee and informing Gerald he'd best take one of the smaller pie pieces. Douglas was still telling anecdotes from some of the ceremonies he'd participated in as best man. All as if nothing was out of the ordinary.

Was it possible no one else noticed how weird tonight had been?

Oh, it had started normally enough—her parents in their usual positions, Jason and Douglas shooting the bull while Savannah dutifully did whatever it was Savannah did in the kitchen. The cooking gene must have skipped Vi, because about the most ambitious dish she prepared was cereal, and even then she had to worry about pouring too much milk and ending up with soggy flakes. Then Neely had shown up with the man who was saving her from Aunt Jo's predictions of "crazy neighborhood cat lady," and introductions were made. Vi wasn't really into older men, but for a guy pushing fifty, Robert wasn't bad. She could definitely see where someone Neely's age would be attracted to him. The evening had followed on cue with Douglas making his small, obnoxious jokes, such as ribbing Vi about her name. A definite source of contention.

It wasn't just the unusual Southern moniker. In a way, *Vidalia* was pretty, even lyrical. But Savannah, the firstborn, had been named after Georgia's very first city and Douglas after the city named for the man who challenged Lincoln for the presidency. The city Cornelia honored was famous for its big red apple statue, which wasn't all that impressive or historically significant, but it was still better than onions, the famed Vidalia produce. She was named for a food that was smelly and known to make people cry.

And they wondered why she seemed bitter compared to Savannah.

Frankly, Vi thought choosing your offspring's names based on a Georgia map was a little bizarre, but it could have been worse. *We could have been Americus, Oglethorpe, Chatsworth and Flowery Branch*—try living down those names on the fifth grade playground. Names, however, had nothing to do with why the evening had been strange.

Savannah, Beth's little debutante, was polished and perfect in almost any social situation, yet she'd been quiet for the first half of the meal. Withdrawn, even. Maybe no one else had noticed because even without Savannah's input, conversation had been lively. But Vi had already been wondering about her sister's silence when she caught Savannah's glances toward her husband. Undisciplined, furtive glances, the kind you shoot at someone even though you've told yourself you won't. Like an ex you've vowed not to notice or maybe a man you love from afar. Or was it more like the glares you throw a boy-friend you were fighting with right before the party, even as you don't want anyone else to know there's something wrong?

Only Savannah didn't look angry, just sad. When she'd briefly mentioned her wedding to Jason, the normal cheer was back in her voice, but Vi, alerted to it now, could spot the despair lurking in her sister's bright gaze. What the hell could possibly be wrong enough in Savannah's life to cause despair? Her entire life had always been as chipper and well-scripted as one of those syrupy feel-good movies televised around Christmas.

The subtle but abrupt change jolted Vi into mild alarm. Savannah's being cheerful and flawless was as natural and unquestioned as sunrise.

Vi had cast a look at Neely, trying to catch her eye and see if her sister had noticed anything wrong. But Neely was busy staring in adoration at her husband-to-be. If Vi wasn't mistaken, they might also have been playing a little innocent footsie under the table.

Then Neely had made a joke later about being glad Vi was in the wedding party because it gave her the chance to make her sister wear something frilly in public. Vi knew better than to buy into the threat—

frills were not Neely's style—and it had dawned on her that Neely was *joking*.

Footsie *and* attempted humor? It was enough to make Vi believe in pod people. Neely had always been the most standoffish of the Mason siblings, at least as far back as Vi could remember. Perhaps love was transforming the bride-to-be, but that left the unsolved mystery of what was bothering Savannah. The obvious answer would seem to be something between her and Jason, except his demeanor was totally relaxed. Besides, accepting that their marriage could be in trouble took more imagination than Vi possessed. And she'd always been quite the creative girl.

As she mulled over the situation that apparently only she had noticed, the irony struck her. Though she prided herself on being able to say just about anything, anywhere, without feeling the least self-conscious, she didn't have the guts to ask her older sister, "Are you okay?"

While the rest of her family said good-night to Robert, Douglas followed Neely to the coat closet. Since she was perfectly capable of retrieving two jackets by herself, she figured this was where he bestowed his brotherly approval.

"He seems like a good guy," Douglas said, confirming her deduction.

"He is." Tonight was proof of that.

"I'm glad you found each other." He shoved his hands in the pockets of his slacks, looking downward. "May you be very happy for many, many years."

Oh, Douglas. She could tell from the note of regret in his voice that he was thinking about his own failed marriage, about Zoe.

There had never been any question that he loved his wife; it had more been a matter of Douglas being insufferable to live with. Growing up with three sisters had probably screwed him up. He tried to joke and charm his way out of every situation, until Zoe had come to the conclusion that he didn't take their relationship seriously. Though no one thought Douglas had cheated on his wife, Neely could understand how watching him use that flirtatious charm on every other female who crossed his path could get old fast. At least one infatuated paralegal had gotten the wrong idea, later to be transferred to another branch of the firm while Douglas shrugged off the awkward situation by teasing that even if the young woman had jumped to a bad conclusion, she had good taste in men.

Her brother cleared his throat. "I do hope you're

together till death do you part and all that morbid romantic stuff, but just as a standard precaution, I could recommend someone really top-notch to handle a prenup at a fair price."

Some brothers would threaten a suitor with "If you ever hurt her, they'll never find your body," but Douglas played to his strength, legal advice. Of the two options, his was more useful. "Thanks. It's a sensible suggestion." She'd already been tossing it around in her mind, just hadn't found the perfect way to ask Robert about it. Mostly, she loved his romantic streak and sometimes even envied the emotion that came so easily to him. But to broach this subject, she needed him to be logical, not sentimental.

Douglas grinned. "You always were sensible. I would have even said predictable, until Sunday. Blew us away with your little announcement."

"Didn't think I could land a husband, huh?"

"Didn't think you'd ever *want* one. You're very…self-contained."

The words came out like the same type of reverse compliment as "she has a good personality." "I have a social life, care about my friends." She cared about her family, too, even though seeing them twice in one week was a bigger dose of Mason than she was used to.

"It wasn't a criticism," he assured her. "Only an observation, although maybe I'm wrong. Turns out, I'm not the expert on women I assumed I was in college."

Just when she was prepared to take his self-deprecating comment as a sign he was maturing, he added an impish, "But that gives me a great excuse to actively study them, right? I'm a strong supporter of a hands-on education."

She rolled her eyes, not wanting to hear the details of his bachelor life. "Spare me. Whether or not you plan to bring a date to the wedding is the extent of what I want to know about you and women."

"A date?" His gaze turned reflective. "I should bring one, shouldn't I?"

"Up to you. But if you show up with some busty bimbo, you'll be hearing about it from Mom later."

"I don't date bimbos," he protested. "Now, a busty litigation secretary on the other hand…"

Neely raised her own hands as if to deflect further conversation, resisting the urge to clap them over her ears.

"You ready to go?" Robert called out, appearing in the hallway outside the front parlor.

"More than." Ignoring the face her brother made at her, she walked toward her fiancé. Her family joined them for one last goodbye.

"I'll see you next weekend?" Savannah asked cheerfully.

Since a groan didn't seem the appropriate response, Neely bit her lower lip to stifle one. She hadn't realized when she'd accepted Robert's proposal that it would result in all this quality family time. "You and Vi can meet me at my apartment." With any luck, Leah would be free to join them, too.

Beth had mentioned over dessert that Neely should start looking at dresses immediately and that it only made sense to take her bridesmaids along. Neely had been shocked her mother didn't want to come, passing up an entire afternoon of offering her opinion, but maybe she needed all her spare time to plan the engagement party she'd announced she was throwing. A big barbecue where family and friends could meet the groom-to-be. She'd insisted Robert write down his parents' phone number so Beth could call them next week about attending. Neely would have met them by then—hopefully she'd leave a good enough impression to counteract anything her mother said.

Frankly, Beth was no more outspoken than any of the other women who congregated regularly to get permanents and discuss the state of the world at Lana's Beauty Shop. But judging from Robert's occasional starts of surprise tonight, Gwen Walsh of Vermont might phrase her opinions differently. Or less often.

Inside her car, which Robert had offered to drive, Neely shot him a mock glare. "You know, it used to be, when I left my parents' house, I could get away with a quick, 'see everyone next month.' Now it seems that for every trip here I take, I'm making two or three more appointments to see them again soon. I blame you."

He laughed. "Well, I *would* point out that some of us from smaller families and with world-traveling parents might envy that kind of, um, closeness. But I have to admit, as nice as your family is, they are exhausting. It's hard to keep pace with your mother in a conversation, yet I was afraid if my attention wandered, I might accidentally agree to something like a new religion or trading in my car for a different model without even realizing she'd talked me into it."

"If I said you get used to it, I'd be lying."

"Maybe I will." Grinning, he dropped his hand from the steering wheel to clasp hers. "I could surprise you."

"You usually do." She'd been stunned when he first kissed her, even more stunned by her own passionate response. *Passionate* wasn't an adjective she would normally apply to herself, unless describing one of her heartfelt lectures about the perils of financial mismanagement. She'd aimed several of those at Vi.

Robert's genuine affection for Neely still occasionally caught her by surprise, although she was adjusting. To her own feelings, as well, finding it easier to make the odd romantic gesture without feeling self-conscious. Nonetheless, while they'd acknowledged their love for each other, his marriage proposal had come as a total surprise.

"You look so serious," he commented.

"Aren't you supposed to be watching the *road?*"

He made a production of leaning forward in his seat, keeping his gaze locked on the dark road that lay beyond the windshield. "Better?"

"Yes, thank you."

"Good. Now are you going to tell me what's on your mind?"

"You." Her thoughts didn't exactly tumble out with ease, but hadn't she just assured herself she was getting better at the whole intimacy thing? "I was…I'm lucky. To have you. I wasn't expecting to fall in love. Maybe I didn't exactly buy Aunt Jo's predicted future of cats and scared neighborhood kids, but—"

"Excuse me?"

"Nothing. My family's overreaction to me being single. And even though I didn't agree with them, I couldn't quite picture myself with Savannah's perfect marriage and family in the burbs, either. I wasn't sure *what* my future was, and that's tough to admit for someone who plans as carefully as I do." Her cheeks warmed. She sounded like some badly written For The One I Love greeting card. "I'm going to stop now, before I feel any more stupid."

"It didn't sound stupid, Cornelia." Someone who didn't know him well would have missed the subtle teasing note interjected at the end of his otherwise sincere sentence.

She smirked, suspecting he'd used her full name to rescue her from an uncomfortably sappy moment. "Since we're contemplating until death do us part, it's only fair to warn you that you'll live longer if you don't call me that."

"What about puddin' bear? Honeykins?"

"Only if you want to be called Snugglepuss," she cautioned.

"Except it would bother you far more than me, so I think we both know that's an empty threat. Can we at least agree that neither of us want to be called the Walsons?"

"Done." But they also had more complicated decisions to discuss. The twenty-minute drive back to her place was as good a time as any to bring it up, so she started with something simple. Whether he eventually agreed they needed a prenuptial agreement or not, he *had* to agree they needed a place to call home. "Since we're making all sorts of plans tonight, there's something I wanted to ask you about."

"Shoot," he invited, his gaze flicking in her direction.

"Well, after the wedding, we'll be living together…"

"That is how it traditionally works."

She took a deep breath. "Yes, but where?"

"Oh." He grew silent, thoughtful. "I'm happy to have you move into my apartment, if you're interested. It does have more room than yours, and you know I'd like you to think of it as your home as much as mine."

"And if I don't?" Her words came out sharply, an involuntary response to his immediate suggestion that she give up her place while he kept his. "Sorry. I just—are you open to other options?"

"Like sharing *your* apartment?"

"As a for instance. It is conveniently located to work and would cut down your commute."

"It's also smaller." He flashed her a boyish grin. "In case you hadn't noticed, I have a lot of stuff."

"I noticed." She chewed on the inside of her lip. "I guess the third option would be that we find a different place, *our* place."

"I like that idea," he said slowly. "A lot. A place of

ours, one we come into as equals, where we can share our life together."

"Yeah." That sounded nice—romantic, logical and the perfect first step for the rest of their lives together.

CHAPTER 5

Her husband would probably describe the quiet in the car as "companionable silence," but Savannah disagreed. To her, it was simply stilted. *Then* say *something*. But she was as tongue-tied as an awkward teenager on a blind date that was tanking. She tried to make a joke out of it, telling herself it was silly that she was nervously casting about for something to say to a man she'd been married to for decades.

Truthfully, though, it was scary.

In a few months, Trent would be out of the house. Would she have something to say then, or would this increasingly routine silence become the norm?

"I love you," she blurted.

Jason cast her a surprised glance. "Love you, too, babe."

Well, that was certainly a conversation starter.

What was wrong with her? She instigated conversations at PTA meetings, charity functions and medical board holiday parties. Plus, they'd just come from a family event that should have provided at least enough fodder for the ride home.

"Robert and Neely seem like a cute couple, don't they?"

"I think your sister's a little long in the tooth for 'cute,' but yeah, they seem compatible."

Compatible? How romantic. And Savannah took offense at her younger sister being called long in the tooth—what did that make *her?* She supposed she could remark on Vi and some of her comments tonight, but Jason had known Vi a long time. Outrageousness from the youngest Mason was commonplace and not all that noteworthy among relatives.

Sighing, she fell back on their familiar unbreakable common bond. "So, looks like our youngest is going to be a Tar Heel." Trent had recently announced that he'd decided on North Carolina for college, but she and Jason hadn't really discussed it yet. She pushed away thoughts of how little they'd discussed lately.

At least it was closer than Philadelphia, where Adam attended Penn. Her pride that he'd been accepted didn't keep her from missing him. "I suppose it was too much to hope that one of our boys would go to school in-state."

Jason chuckled. "Is that what's wrong with you?"

Though his tone was more casual than critical, the question stung. "What do you mean, wrong with me?"

"Well, you haven't quite been yourself. You've seemed nee—vulnerable."

Maybe he'd been paying more attention to her than she'd realized. "You never asked if something was bothering me."

"Figured you'd bring up whatever it was when you were ready, and looks like I was right. Do you want to talk about Trent moving out?" Another chuckle. "Can't say I think it will change much. I'll tell you the boys are able to take care of themselves, that you did a good job raising them and shouldn't make yourself crazy worrying, you'll agree, then you'll worry anyway."

"Ah. It does sound like a waste of a conversation." Knowing there was some truth in what he said, she wondered why she felt so ticked off all of a sudden. He hadn't *meant* to sound dismissive and vaguely condescending. Maybe he'd be less so if his whole existence would change next fall when Trent moved away, but Jason's important medical career would continue just the same as it always had.

Silence descended once again, even less companionable than before. Savannah was determined not to sit here stewing. She'd always been upbeat, interested in finding solutions. If she and Jason weren't as close as they'd once been, why not take steps to change that?

"Want to do something this weekend?" she asked.

"Like what?"

"Um…I think there's an international ballet troupe performing at the Fox?"

He shuddered. "Why don't you take a friend, have a girls' day out?"

Which sort of defeated the whole *them* doing something together idea. Was it her fault baseball season hadn't started and ballet was more convenient than the Braves?

Before she could amend her suggestion to an action-movie matinee, he was reminding her, "You know I'm playing golf with the guys from the Suwannee practice on Sunday, right? And aren't you going to be wedding dress shopping all day Saturday?"

"Yes, I guess I am."

"Another weekend, then," he pronounced.

Right. They had lots of future weekends looming ahead, so there was no reason for this strange desperation knotting her gut. *Get a hold of yourself.* For all she knew, there was nothing wrong between them at all—*he* certainly didn't seem to think so—and she could just be having some kind of hormonal reaction. Though he would never think of revealing any confidential patient specifics, Jason had been mentioning more women of a certain age lately. She suspected he was trying to prepare her for some changes to come, unable to completely separate his doctor self from the husband. Maybe all she needed to improve her outlook were some herbal supplements.

When Jason shot her an absent smile, she returned it optimistically before they lapsed back into silence. He reached out to hit the button for talk radio, but she didn't exactly consider that an improvement.

"My first act as maid of honor, and I'm letting you down already!"

Neely laughed into the phone. "Don't worry, it's not like we'll have to cancel the wedding because of this."

"You're sure?" Leah asked. "I mean, not about canceling the wedding, but that you don't mind?"

Well, Neely might not be *relishing* the thought of spending hours alone with her two sisters, but she wasn't angry. Especially since she knew Leah would benefit from the extra cash. "If they need you at work, you should be there. We can look at dresses without you—of course, you have no one to blame but yourself if you end up having to wear some low-cut gown adorned with feathers." Grinning, she doodled something appropriately horrid on the notepad on her kitchen table.

"Your bluff doesn't scare me. Savannah oozes good taste. She wouldn't let you stick your attendants in something tacky."

True. But, as Neely got off the phone, she bristled at the idea of anyone not "letting" her do something. She finished the last of her coffee and washed the mug out at the sink, then rubbed the counters down with as much irritation as antibacterial cleanser. Wasn't this supposed to be *her* wedding? Apparently none of the women in her family had received that memo. Even Aunt Carol had called last night to ensure her suggestions were added to the growing list.

Carol was her youngest aunt, and she and Neely got along well. Having five children, including triplets, had given Carol a thrifty mindset an accountant could appreciate. Sometimes, however, Carol took her cost-savings to an extreme. Neely had promised to think over her aunt's suggestion of placing a bulk order for white-frosted cupcakes that could be decoratively arranged and saving herself the expense of a wedding cake. But she'd refused Carol's offer to loan her and Robert her daughter's old Cinderella motorized bubble blower so that they didn't have to buy individual bottles of wedding bubbles for guests.

"You and Rupert could run through the usual post-ceremony shower of bubbles at no cost whatsoever."

"*Robert*, Aunt Carol. And if we decide to go the bubble route, I'm sure we can find a way to afford it, thanks." Something that didn't involve a sticky garage sale toy perched on a stool at the top of the church steps.

"You're probably right, dear. Besides, you haven't heard my idea for how to save money on flowers yet. With all the excess cash you won't need for a florist, bubbles won't be any problem!"

It was only after Neely had bid her aunt good night, sighing in relief as she hung up the phone, that she'd really taken in how quiet her apartment was. In the past few months, she'd grown accustomed to sharing her evenings with Robert. But he'd told her he was working late and wouldn't be coming over, which made good sense, especially with her sisters arriving in the morning for a day of shopping. Still…had his decision stemmed partly from their talks about finding a new home together? Was he nervous, savoring his final, numbered days in his own residence?

Or maybe that was just her.

The sudden knock distracted her from feeling guilty that she'd enjoyed her night of solitude. She opened the front door and found two women so different from each other that a stranger never would have guessed they were sisters. Savannah was wearing a mint-green sweater set and calf-length skirt, her golden hair pulled back in a French braid that looked like too much trouble for a Saturday morning; Vi, on the other hand, looked as if her styling regimen had consisted of running her fingers through her short platinum hair until it stood on end. She wore one of her ubiquitous T-shirts with a sarcastic slogan—Beth had outlawed the ones using profanity from Sunday dinners, but Vi seemed to have plenty of others—over black jeans and Doc Marten boots.

Savannah met Neely's gaze with an air of apology. "I tried to get her to change when I picked her up."

Vi shrugged. "What does it matter what I'm wearing?"

"We'll be going to some nice stores," Savannah pointed out, although Neely could have told her that appealing to Vi's worries about what other people thought wouldn't get her anywhere.

"Neely's the potential client, not me."

"But we may try on bridesmaid's dresses," Savannah said in the same tone she'd used on her boys when they were troublesome toddlers. Frustration rolled off her in waves, hinting what the ride over had been like.

"In which case I'll be *removing* these clothes and putting *on* others." Vi echoed her sister's exaggerated patience right back at her. "So again, who cares what I'm wearing?"

Savannah rolled her hazel eyes. "Right. Why try on

a dress with somewhat appropriate shoes and accessories when we could see how it looks with combat boots and junky jewelry instead? Maybe that's the look Neely's going for! Hey, I know—for the wedding, we could all get matching tattoos that say Bite Me."

The retort shocked a burst of laughter from Neely. Vi just stood on the small concrete slab of a front porch, gaping.

"I'm sorry." Hands clapped to her cheeks, Savannah strode inside. "That was inappropriate. I don't know what's... It won't happen again."

"There's nothing junky about my jewelry," Vi muttered as she passed Neely. She fingered a choker that appeared to be beads woven into strands of straw. "I made this, you know. She doesn't have to be bitchy just because some of us like necklaces with more individuality than some strand of pearls Jason gave her."

This day just had Big Damn Fun written all over it.

Savannah stood between the living room and kitchen, glancing around with approval. "So clean. You should have seen the mess *her*—"

"Remind me again why I'm giving up one of my only free Saturdays for this abuse," Vi interrupted with a menacing glare.

Looking more alarmed than apologetic, Savannah backpedaled, redirecting her helpful criticism. "Not that your place couldn't use a few personal touches, Neely, to warm it up. A little potpourri, a shadow box with some keepsakes. Once you and Robert are married, those homey accents really make a difference."

Neely wanted to ask how cinnamon-scented twigs could possibly affect their life together, but decided her energy was better spent attacking the chore at hand. "So, are we all ready to go?"

Vi grinned. "Must we leave so soon? I was finally starting to enjoy the conversation."

The ride to the first store was a sea of shifting alliances. When Vi's choice of radio stations in the SUV was vetoed by her older sisters, she muttered that she really had to get her own car; Neely retorted that such a purchase would require some financial responsibility and careful thought. Later, when Savannah asked what time the wedding would be, explaining that different dresses were worn for morning, afternoon or evening ceremonies, Neely and Vi exchanged pained glances of commiseration.

As Savannah navigated a parking space, Neely admitted that she wasn't entirely sure about the time. "The church office said they thought they could work us in the last weekend in June, but they're calling back to confirm specifics. Let's just find a dress I like and if it turns out not to meet Emily Post's time-of-day guide-lines…well, we won't invite Emily to the wedding."

Hurt shimmered in Savannah's gaze. "You're being sarcastic."

"Actually, she was probably sincere about not inviting a dead chick," Vi interjected from the backseat.

"I was trying to help," Savannah continued. "I realize *you* don't care about—"

"I'm sorry," Neely said quickly. It hadn't been her intention to wound Savannah. Maybe she had been a smidge sarcastic, but half an hour of sitting in traffic with her two sisters could do that to a person. "I know you're here to assist, and I appreciate it. Really."

Savannah nodded, but said nothing as she climbed out of the car.

"Does she seem okay to you this morning?" Vi whispered, unbuckling her seat belt but not reaching for the door handle. "I thought her normal policy was to take the moral high ground and ignore sarcasm. She's normally so serene, but she's snapped at me at least three times."

"You sure you didn't deserve it?"

"Not the point. I'm just saying she seems, I don't know, fragile lately."

An apt description, Neely mused as they walked toward an ornate entrance flanked by festive window displays of gowns and bridal bouquets. While Savannah was undeniably the most feminine and superficially delicate of the three Mason sisters, she'd also opted for natural childbirth—twice—and had successfully raised rough-and-tumble sons. Beneath her soft-spoken, perfectly polished exterior, she had as much grit as anyone in the family. Right now, however, beneath the refined veneer, she seemed almost brittle.

Come to think of it, she reminded Neely a little of Leah, in the days following her friend's divorce. The comparison startled her, especially since the two women led such different lives.

With Leah, Neely would have at least asked if something was wrong and if she could help. Asking Savannah those same questions seemed both invasive and silly. Neely couldn't imagine anything wrong in Savannah's life, but her sister definitely gave off the vibe that if something *were* amiss, she could fix it without involving others. It struck Neely that, in a less obvious way, Savannah could be as private as she herself was. Still, as Neely followed her sisters inside, she vowed to show more gratitude today. And she'd try to head off Vi's snarkier comments, as well.

A saleswoman materialized instantly, with only a waft

of distinguished perfume as a warning. "Good morning, ladies! I'm Fallon. How may I assist you today?"

Vi jabbed a finger at Neely. "She's getting married."

"Congratulations! When's the happy day?"

"June," Neely answered. "So I need a dress."

"Certainly. And is there a particular style you'd like to see? Sheath, princess, mermaid?"

"Um…" Why had she thought this would be as easy as going into a store and looking around until she found a dress she liked? Except for those displayed in the window, she didn't even *see* any dresses in the front room, which was decorated like an upscale coffee shop, with fussy little chairs clustered around gilt-edged circular tables.

Savannah caught her eye and, after allowing herself a small smile, turned to Fallon. "If you'll excuse us for a few minutes, we're going to sit down and thumb through a couple of the books."

"Of course, of course. Can I get you anything while you're looking? Water, espresso?"

After politely declining her offer, the three sisters moved to sit at one of the tables. Savannah immediately shoved aside a couple of the French-titled magazines on top of the stack. Catching sight of a frightening example of haute couture, Neely silently applauded her sister's decision.

"You really didn't prepare for this at all?" Savannah asked, sounding amused.

"Prepare? How do you prepare to shop?"

Vi snorted. "Maybe last time you were at a supermarket you noticed the racks of approximately eight hundred bridal magazines they sell for people just like you?"

Ah, so now it was time for them to gang up on her. Fair enough. "I did flip through one, and trust me, it was *not* for people like me." Articles about creating personalized scrapbooks for your bridesmaids, pictorial essays on Caribbean honeymoon resorts and dozens of glossy photos of thin radiant brides who looked all of seventeen, smiling at tuxedoed men and cute little ring bearers posed on adjoining pages. She had seen one article on "second marriage traditions," where the fictional bride in the accompanying picture looked a ripe old twenty-three.

"Maybe we could ask Fallon if they have a *Brides Over Forty* magazine," Vi suggested.

"Ha ha." On second thought, was there such a publication?

"Stand up," Savannah said. "I assume you're going with a traditional wedding?"

Seemed a safe bet, considering her conservative life and personality. Neely sometimes wondered if she'd simply been born this way—an apparent anomaly in her outgoing family—or if she'd just decided young she couldn't measure up to Savannah and was better off fading into the woodwork to avoid unfavorable comparison. "Yeah."

"Damn." Vi glanced up from a picture of what looked like a gypsy fantasy dress, with multicolored sequins adorning the white bodice and a gauzy skirt cut at jagged, layered angles. "So I can't talk you into something like this?"

Since she and Robert had decided on a church wedding and would not be getting married at the annual Georgia Renaissance Festival, Neely gave a quick shake of her head.

Taking her consultant duties seriously, Savannah circled Neely, scrutinizing her. "We can narrow down the selections based on your body type. You're about average height, decent build. Don't wear anything that hugs your butt too tightly, though."

Great, now she'd spend the ceremony self-conscious about standing with her back to a roomful of people, giving them all a good look at the rear end that had done a little spreading with age. Neely knew she wasn't fat, but she also knew that if they were here shopping for twenty-six-year-old Vi, they'd have a wider variety of flattering options.

"A little top-heavy," Savannah commented objectively.

Neely had always been the bustiest of the three sisters—barring the periods during Savannah's pregnancies when her chest had blown up to resemble a couple of cantaloupes—but it wasn't something she emphasized. The only good thing cleavage had ever done was attract Daniel Turner in college. This had been during her rebellious phase, out on her own for the first time and resentful over years of being in Savannah's golden shadow. Prompted by her attraction to a campus bad boy, Neely had flirted with living on the wild side. The brief and uncharacteristic urge had died when Daniel dumped her, humiliating her and leaving her ashamed at how she'd given up her virginity, which she knew full well he'd bragged about to other guys.

Neely had been too embarrassed to tell anyone in her family about the short but painful relationship, especially when she could all but hear her mother's disapproval in her head. On the other hand, making as big a mistake as Daniel early in her adult life had taught her a lesson. That's why she could call attracting him in the first place a "good" thing; their breakup had put her firmly back on the straight and narrow.

Done cataloging Neely's physical attributes, Savannah moved on to suggested styles. "Something slightly off-shoulder might be flattering without making your arms look bulky."

"My arms are bulky?" At least it gave her something to worry about besides an ass the size of the East Coast.

"Your arms are fine," Savannah said. "But something with tiny cap sleeves might not show them to their best advantage and I'm thinking long sleeves are out for a sweltering June."

Neely considered the few preliminary hot flashes she'd suffered through and the fact that she'd already run her air-conditioning this year. "You're thinking right."

"Great. I have several ideas about what will look nice on you. Why don't we let Fallon know we're ready for her? We'll find you the perfect dress—if not here, then somewhere else. Every bride deserves to be beautiful on her wedding day."

Savannah certainly had been. Though her wedding had been simple, especially by Southern debutante standards, her gown had been like something from a fairy tale. Blinding, virginal white with lacy accents, a full Scarlett O'Hara petticoat, and little puffed sleeves. *I would have looked like Bo Peep on crack in that thing.*

"Um, Savannah, I think ivory's more appropriate for me than bright white and nothing too…fussy, okay?"

As though reading her mind, Savannah grinned. "You mean nothing like mine?"

"Well, you were a much younger bride. Maybe women over forty should limit the number of ruffles they wear in public. And—"

"Don't worry. I know you're not me. Your wedding will be different." She walked off to find Fallon, so Neely couldn't be sure—her ears must be deceiving her—but it sounded as if her sister also muttered, "Hopefully your marriage will be, too."

Vi huffed out an exasperated breath. "I can't believe this. Three thousand poufy white dresses, and we can't find one that looks good on you?"

"Thanks a lot," Neely said dryly.

Savannah scoffed, "She isn't trying on any of the ones that are white and puffy, remember?"

Okay, Vi conceded silently, maybe her sister was trying on cream-colored dresses with A-line skirts, but they still lacked imagination and all basically looked alike. As if echoing her discontent, her stomach rumbled, the noise exaggerated by the fitting room's acoustics.

Perhaps food would boost her mood and blood sugar levels. "I know we're on a quest here, Fellowship of the Wedding Gown and all, but do you think we might stop long enough to have lunch somewhere?"

"Oh, nice," Neely muttered as she struggled free of

the latest dress with Savannah's help. "I was spilling out of that last one like some doughy pirate wench and you want me to go *eat?*"

"You're not overweight," Savannah fussed. "Some of these dresses are just sized a little differently."

"They were sized by a sadist." The increasingly cranky bride-to-be retrieved her discarded blouse. She'd recovered from her earlier inhibitions about changing in front of an audience.

At the first store, when Savannah, Vi and Fallon had all crowded in to help Neely put the dress on, suggest possible alterations and offer opinions, she'd grumbled about her half-dressed state and a distinct lack of privacy. Savannah had dismissed her with, "Oh, come crying to me when *you* have a lactation specialist trying to help your newborn latch on and a doctor's checking to make sure your episiotomy is healing correctly while your in-laws are standing there telling you how proud they are to have a grandson. Until then, stand still and suck in so I can get this zipped."

Despite actually admiring the acerbic retorts, Vi was more convinced than ever that something was wrong with her oldest sister. Until recently, the only emotions Savannah publicly displayed were dutiful devotion to their parents and glowing pride for her own family. Vi had often found herself waiting for the day her sister snapped—and secretly looking forward to it. Yet now she was unsettled. Though Savannah showed no signs of a psychotic episode, she vacillated between moments of near-weepy nostalgia and uncharacteristic snippiness. What happened to just shaking her head in quiet disapproval?

Neely was worried, too. She kept darting quizzical glances when Savannah wasn't looking, as if searching for something.

"Lunch is an excellent idea," Savannah said. "I wouldn't mind a bite…and the chance to get off my feet for a little while."

Vi smirked. "You should get yourself a pair of combat boots. These babies are incredibly comfortable."

Savannah indicated her outfit with a sweep of her left hand. "Yes, I'm sure those clunkers would look just perfect with this."

"You could always buy new clothes while you're at it. Spruce up the old wardrobe a little."

For a second, if Vi didn't know her sister better, it looked as if Savannah might actually be considering the idea.

Oh, Lord, it's worse than I thought. Maybe Savannah was on the verge of some sort of midlife crisis? After all, she would be fifty in a few years. Although Vi razzed her sister about her Stepford suburbanite look, the thought of her suddenly showing up in a pleather skirt with a few henna streaks in her hair was absolutely terrifying. Vi took a mental oath not to say anything further that could push her in that direction.

Wouldn't that be the ultimate irony? For someone in her family to take her advice after years of dismissing her input with rolled eyes and the occasional "Vidalia Jean!"

Not that you ever gave anyone a compelling reason for taking your advice. Privately, Vi could admit that her life was something of a mess, characterized by a lot of ex-boyfriends and massive student loans. It had taken her three degree changes to find a major that didn't bore her to tears, and now she had an extremely practical Masters in Art History. No doubt her Masters in Philosophy, once completed, would be just the useful instrument she needed to finally land a Fortune 500 job, she thought sardonically.

Anyone who knew her could accurately predict she'd quit an office job within her first week and would need a major shopping expedition to last that long. The navy suit Neely had given her as a graduation present was the sum total of Vi's business attire. It had taken up permanent residence in the back of the closet, original tags still attached. Currently, she juggled an early-morning front desk job at a gym that catered to students, fifteen hours a week in an offbeat bookstore and a few shifts at a hole-in-the-wall that aspired to be a nightclub. The crowd was small but regular and Vi made decent tips while getting to hear some promising undiscovered bands.

Once again fully dressed, Neely stepped into a pair of tan mules. "All right, so where are we eating?"

Vi pursed her lips. "I know this funky little Thai—"

"There's a place one street over that makes great salads," Savannah said, obviously not a fan of pad Thai noodles and green curry. "And if you're in the mood for seafood, they always have terrific fish specials."

"You had me at 'one street over,'" Neely said. "Anything close gets my vote. Shopping for a wedding gown is exhausting."

True. Vi hadn't even tried anything on and she was fatigued.

Twenty minutes later, they were seated in a gated outdoor courtyard, enjoying the relatively warm day.

Vi loved spring, the sunshine that seemed to blossom over the city in a peaceful, generous mood before the punishing heat of summer. Of course, not every day was sunny. Spring storms could blow in with the dark, vindictive speed of a scorned woman, but she loved those rainy tempests, too.

"If I ever get married, it will probably be in March," she mused. "Or April."

Both of her sisters stared.

"What?" Her comment wasn't that random, considering they'd spent the day discussing wedding plans.

"I'm just trying to picture you as someone's wife," Savannah finally said. "It's a little mind-boggling."

Vi flashed an audacious grin. "Well, I probably wouldn't run right out and sign a mortgage on my very own picket fence, but I do like the idea of sex being so readily available." She was kidding, of course. Anytime she wanted sex, she had only to call Brendan. He was good in bed, but relationships were always more exciting in the beginning. Wondering when you'd do it for the first time, the rush of exploring each other and getting to know specific turn-ons.

"That's the point of marriage, all right." Savannah's voice dripped sarcasm. "One big orgy."

"I can't picture you having sex," Vi admitted. Talk about mind-boggling.

Savannah made a face. "Don't tell me you try."

"I doubt she means the actual visual," Neely interrupted with a laugh. "I think she means, you know, *you*. Having sex."

"I've been pregnant twice," Savannah said, somewhat defensively.

"We're not saying we don't believe you've ever had

it," Vi tried to explain. "It's just difficult to imagine you swept away by passion." Sex was probably a very polite matter in the Carter household.

Instead of more defensiveness, Savannah's gaze drew dreamy, her lips parting in a slow, soft smile that took ten years off her face. "You'd be surprised. Naturally, Jason and I waited until we were married—"

"Naturally," both of her sisters chorused.

"—but those first few years…I'm not sure how he kept up the energy, what with medical school and interning. And I was pretty impressive myself, considering how much a newborn can wear you out. It was just luck that Adam and Trent have a few years between them. As often as Jason and I used to go at it—"

"Whoa. Okay, there. My bad." Vi was stunned.

For Savannah, that had been the equivalent of a graphic letter to *Penthouse*. Or at least a racy note to *Redbook*. Not that Savannah had said anything shocking—Vi and her girlfriends had far more candid conversations—just, this was Savannah, who'd been as much mother as sister to her.

Neely was quiet, not touching her salad. "You said 'those first few years.' Does that mean things are different now?"

Savannah laughed. Tittered, really, sounding as nervous as someone about to be caught in a lie. "Naturally things are different. It wouldn't be called the honeymoon phase if it was forever."

"Granted. But…everything is all right? Between you and Jason?"

Staring down at her plate, Savannah opened her mouth, then closed it again. The unanswered question stretched across the white tablecloth until it became a response of its own.

"He's wonderful," she finally said.

The waiter had shown more conviction about the day's fish special.

"Our marriage is wonderful," Savannah pressed on with a determined smile. "We just aren't twenty anymore."

There was an awkward pause that left Vi feeling oddly guilty for being the only one at the table under thirty. Bizarre, considering how rarely she felt self-conscious. She forced a smile at her oldest sister. "Hey, in a few months, Trent will be out of the house, so who knows? Maybe you and Jason can use the alone time to recapture that down-and-dirty newlywed zeal."

Clearly the wrong thing to say—Savannah looked perilously close to tears.

Vi babbled on desperately, "And there are things you can do, or use, to make sex more like it was when you were in your twenties. Like obviously Kegels, since you've had two babies and…" Afraid she was only making things worse, Vi redirected her suggestions to Neely instead. That way Savannah got the benefit of the advice without anyone making her feel old. "You're about to make a monogamous commitment. Why not make it the most exciting commitment it can be? You can order Ben-Wa balls to help tighten—"

Neely spewed sweet tea. "Savannah was right, the food here is lovely. Why don't we all enjoy our lunches for the next five minutes and *not say anything?*"

Probably a good plan.

Still, Vi couldn't help thinking that she'd only been trying to help. Funny, that was what Savannah had said this morning when Neely had made her sarcastic Emily Post response. It painted such a clear picture of their sibling roles. Savannah, offering assistance in the form of traditional wedding etiquette, and then there was Vi. Making sex toy recommendations.

Neely would be perfectly happy never to try on another wedding dress so long as she lived—unfortunately, yesterday had been a flop. While the search had turned up nothing more than blisters and bizarre behavior in her siblings, at least she was free from dress hunting today due to prior plans. She was officially meeting Mr. and Mrs. Walsh.

In just a few months, she'd *be* Mrs. Walsh.

The thought gave her a pleasant tingle. She'd secretly wondered if enjoying the last two days without Robert was abnormal for a bride-to-be, but she'd also missed him. Seeing his familiar grin as she opened her front door made her realize how much.

"Hey." He leaned in for a quick kiss hello. Quick, but thorough. When his lips moved against hers, a little *ping* ricocheted through her stomach.

"Hey yourself." She smiled in greeting as he released her.

"You look nice." Then he winked. "Well, maybe except for the smudged lipstick, but I guess that's my fault."

She made a mental note to reapply in the car. "Thank you. I…wasn't sure what to wear." She'd changed clothes three times, first pulling on a skirt, even though she rarely wore them. Must be Savannah's lingering influence. But she'd felt foreign in the conspicuously feminine outfit she'd selected and changed to be more comfortable. Except her second choice leaned too far into casual, giving her a slouchy look more appropriate to loafing around the house than meeting Robert's parents.

Now that she thought about it, her first selection had been a little too Savannah, her second a little too

Vi. Luckily, her third choice, a pretty scallop-necked top paired with loose, flowing slacks was all Neely. *Ah, just right*.

But Robert didn't need to know about her brief wardrobe neurosis, so she kept it to herself as she locked her apartment door behind them. He held her hand as they walked to his car, and when he gave her fingers a quick squeeze of encouragement, she thought he must know how nervous she was. It was silly, really, to be concerned. In the six months she'd dated Robert, her path had never crossed his parents', so it wasn't as if she was expecting these people to have any bearing on her daily life. Still…

"How long a drive is it?" she asked as he started the car.

He laughed. "We haven't even left the parking lot, Neely. It's a little soon for 'are we there yet?'"

"I guess I thought making conversation would help me ignore these butterflies in my stomach."

His grin made him look entirely too pleased with himself.

"What? You think it's funny that I'm nervous?"

"It's sweet. You have to admit, of the two of us, you're not really the emotional one."

"I have emotions," she muttered, but she knew what he meant.

Robert was more likely to go with a gut reaction, while she stood back with a detached eye, analyzing and considering. He'd teased her the morning after his proposal that he'd been afraid she'd want to go home and sleep on it, taking the night to deliberate. What she would have felt corny telling him was that she'd had forty-five years to think it over, to ponder whether or not she wanted to be alone. She had all that time and several failed relationships to compare against what she felt with Robert; she didn't need a colored pie graph to show her how much happier she was now.

He threw her a conversational rope. "So, how did yesterday go? Find a dress you can model for me after lunch?"

"Nope, no dress." Some might argue that his seeing her in it before the wedding was bad luck anyway, but Neely figured that was the least of a marriage's potential hurdles. "I have a comparatively light day Tuesday, so I'm leaving work early to try again."

Savannah had pushed for her to take the entire day off, but Neely had balked. It had helped that Vi had her part-time job at that weird bookstore in the morning and couldn't make it then. Neely had refrained from asking Vi if she was going to find a real career once she'd finished this latest degree. It wasn't that Neely meant to be judgmental—obviously Vi had found she was good at school, and hey who doesn't appreciate knowledge?—but Vi needed to get serious. She needed a real job, one with health benefits besides "the bouncer walks me home at night so I don't worry about muggers and stuff." Beneath her attitude, the girl was bright and could be making decent money which might even lead to a decent place to live. But Neely bit her tongue whenever possible.

She figured Vi got enough nagging from their mother and Savannah. More would probably just make the stubborn young woman dig her heels in deeper. Besides, Neely knew what it was like to need to rebel after getting out from under Beth's thumb and Savannah's shadow. The difference was, *she'd* outgrown it and moved on with her life.

"So another day with the sisters?" Robert asked.

"Yep."

He sighed. "In some ways, I envy you."

Because he sounded so wistful, she tried teasing him. "You have a yen to try on dresses? That's definitely the type of thing I should know about *before* the wedding."

"Nut." He flashed her a grin. "You know I meant the whole only-child thing."

And he didn't think there were times she wished she came from a slightly smaller family? "Well, on the bright side, it probably allowed you more quality time and attention from your parents." Not that Neely would have known what to do with more attention from Beth. There was an overwhelming thought.

Robert's mouth twisted. "Attention from my parents."

"Did I say something wrong?" He'd never mentioned anything that made her think he didn't get along with them.

"No, it's just…they wanted me to be my own person, independent and capable of making my own mistakes and decisions. They were never the kind to look over my shoulder or give me advice."

A nonmeddling family? Some people had all the luck.

CHAPTER 7

"Well, this is it." Robert pulled the car between the posts of a black iron gate and up the driveway toward a small but lovely house, its vinyl siding so clean the house appeared new. The yard matched the home—not large, but perfectly manicured, a tiny square of jewel-green lawn. Well-shaped shrubs and rosebushes flanked the front door.

Once out of the car, they followed a path of decorative red stones to the doorbell. This was so different from the Mason home, which needed to be repainted and sprawled awkwardly due to an addition previous owners had constructed decades ago. Beth and Gerald's yard spanned a full acre, decorated with magnolia trees that would probably bloom next month. Neely and her siblings had grown up with lots of space to run around, but the necessary maintenance was a bit beyond her parents' current abilities. A hired man cut the lawn for them twice a month, but during rainy times of the year, the grass grew to jungle proportions between visits. Not that it mattered so much now that there were no children playing out in it. Her parents spent most of their time outside on the spacious but rickety wooden wraparound porch.

Robert had mentioned before that this wasn't the house he'd lived in during his high school years. His parents had moved into a newer home with less bedroom space and a smaller kitchen as soon as he'd started college, storing most of his stuff until he graduated. Then they'd told him to come get anything he wanted to keep and donate or scrap the rest. A practical approach, in Neely's opinion. Her mother still had boxes of old toys that were in no condition to be sold as antiques and not close enough to current safety standards to hand over to unsuspecting grandchildren or great-nieces. *Probably all covered in lead-based paint and linked together with tiny plastic choking hazards.*

Neely didn't see anyone through the beveled glass, but after the doorbell chimed, a gravelly voice called out, "Come in, the door's not locked."

She took a deep breath. When Robert had phoned his parents before their cruise to make this date, he'd mentioned he was bringing a woman he'd like them to meet. He hadn't added that by the appointed lunch, he would have proposed to her. Surely they'd be happy with the news, though, right? If they were anything like Neely's family, they would be thinking, "About damn time."

Who was she kidding? If they were like her family, they'd flat out *say*, "About damn time."

Robert opened the door for her, and they passed through a tiled entryway under an arch into an airy living room. There might not be much in the way of square footage, but the high ceiling gave the place a much bigger feel. At the opposite end was a kitchen, the direction from which his parents came.

Mr. Walsh shuffled along with the support of a cane. Despite the stoop of the man's shoulders and increased gray in his thinner hair, Neely could see where Robert got his good looks. His father's smile was still charming and his eyes sharp, the same color as his son's. Mrs. Walsh reached them first. Lightly tanned and rosy-cheeked from her tropical vacation, she looked fantastic. Her hair was a distinguished silver, cut in a soft sleek cloud that framed her face. She could be mistaken for a woman in her fifties, though Neely knew she had recently turned seventy. This was a woman who had taken good physical care of herself.

"Robert!" His mother kissed his cheek, then stepped aside to make room for her husband. "Nice to see you, you're looking well. And this must be your lady friend?"

"Neely Mason," he said, clasping his father's hand in both of his own. "Neely, these are my parents, Gwen and Everett Walsh."

"Pleased to meet you." Neely smiled at them both. "You have a lovely home."

Gwen returned the smile. "Well, it's nothing grand, but it certainly works for us. Especially since we're hardly here."

"My parents are quite the globe-trotters," Robert said.

Everett laughed ruefully. "More pampered seniors' cruises lately than backpacking trips through Europe, but we try to see as much as we can."

"I've yet to go on a cruise or visit Europe," Neely said. "So you're way ahead of me."

"Maybe later Dad can show us the video he's shot of all the European castles they've visited."

"Don't even joke about that." Gwen shuddered. "Neely, it would be the longest eight hours of your life. It would have been more if he'd remembered to charge the camcorder batteries. If you like castles, I suggest you just look at the photos I took. Much quicker."

Neely followed the direction her future mother-in-law was pointing and saw a cluster of photographs hanging over the sofa. It was a gorgeous assortment—

panoramic shots in vivid color alongside smaller black-and-white close-ups of castle architecture.

"These are fantastic. And all of them are your work?"

Gwen nodded. "Those are from Germany, about eight years ago. Photography was just one of my little hobbies."

"They could pass for professional photos."

"I like her," Gwen told her son. "You should've brought her around sooner."

"Maybe Robert hasn't known her that long," her husband suggested.

"A few years, actually," Robert said. "We work together."

"Oh? How nice. From everything Robert's told us, Becker's a good company to be with," Gwen said. "Would either of you like something to drink? We have bottled water, soft drinks and iced tea."

"Tea would be great, thank you," Neely said. "Is there anything I can do to help?"

"If you'd like to put ice in the glasses. I have a deli tray I'll set on the table, and everyone can make their own sandwiches. Hope it's okay that lunch is so low-key. I rarely cook anymore for just Everett and me."

Mr. Walsh cleared his throat, winking when he had Neely's attention. "Don't let her fool you. She rarely cooked before, either."

"Sandwiches sound fine," Neely said, thinking she

was practically too nervous to eat. Did the Walshes already have a good idea of why Robert had brought her here today, or would it come as a shock to them? Good thing they both looked so hale and hearty; as a general rule, shocking people in their seventies might be a bad idea.

She helped Mrs. Walsh fill crystal glasses that matched the tea pitcher already on the table. Robert unwrapped bread and pulled condiments from the re-frigerator as he asked his parents about the trip.

"It was all right," his mother answered, "but I think I liked that last cruise line we used a little better. We'll probably book them again for a trip this summer."

Neely shot a glance in Robert's direction, wonder-ing if this was the segue he'd use to tell them they might want to be in town the final Saturday in June. According to the message the church secretary left on her answering machine yesterday, she and Robert would be getting married at three that afternoon.

But he chose not to deliver the news while he had his head in the fridge trying to find the reduced-fat mayonnaise his mother insisted was in there some-where. Instead he merely asked in a teasing tone, "So did you bring me any souvenirs?"

"Don't we always?" his father asked. "Where did we put that, dear?"

Gwen found a small plastic bag and handed it to their son. Robert pulled out a clock shaped like a turtle. On the face, small but bright letters proclaimed It's Always A Good Time In The Caymans. An interesting decor choice.

Robert laughed. "Thanks. I think I'll hang it over the hula girl lamp."

The fact that he owned such a lamp was news to Neely, so she doubted she had to worry about these souvenirs being prominently displayed in their residence.

They all found their seats, and Neely gratefully accepted the glass of tea Robert poured for her. She took a sip, then choked on the unexpectedly bitter taste. Her eyes belatedly registered the packets of sugar Robert had set near her spoon. Unsweetened tea—definitely not a Southern concept. Most places here, dumping in a cup of sugar was just part of the brewing process. She tore open the white packets and was in the process of vigorously stirring when Robert cleared his throat.

"Mom, Dad, I know our Christmas visit was pretty hectic, what with your getting ready to head to that resort in Phoenix for a month, but you may remember that I mentioned I was seeing someone." He gestured toward Neely. "Since then, I have fallen very much in love with her. Luckily, she returns those feelings and just last weekend agreed to marry me."

The Walshes both spoke at once. "Well, that's lovely," Gwen was saying, just as Everett said that news like this called for something more than tea for a toast.

"Not that we have any champagne," he said with a quick glance at his wife. "*Do* we have any champagne?"

"No, but the Bransens gave us a nice cabernet for our anniversary that we haven't opened yet."

"You're thinking of the Millers," Everett argued. "The Bransens gave us that glass bird you said represents happiness."

"Well," Robert said, "whoever gave you the wine, would you like me to—"

"Oh, yes, yes, sorry." Mr. Walsh reached for his cane, but Robert placed his hand on his father's arm.

"Just tell me where, Dad. I can get it."

After he'd left the table, Gwen beamed at Neely. "This is delightful news. You'll tell us as soon as you know the wedding date?"

"The last Saturday in June, actually. The church confirmed yesterday."

"You must both be so excited," Gwen said with a happy sigh.

"Yes, ma'am. My family's thrilled, too. We told them about the engagement this week, and my mother insisted on throwing an informal party in April. We'd love for you to join us."

"Everett and I will check our schedules and see if we're available."

Neely had the absent thought that in her family, there was only one schedule—her mother's. The Professor showed up when and where his wife commanded.

As Robert returned with the bottle, Everett informed Neely that she seemed like a wonderful girl. *Girl?* She grinned. It was the type of comment Vi routinely condemned as sexist and patronizing, but Neely didn't much mind terms that made her sound young.

After the toast, Robert mentioned his and Neely's plans to start house-hunting. She was excited about the prospect, but it was daunting, as well. Just searching for a dress was draining, and she wasn't planning to live in that for the next twenty years.

"I am looking forward to having a mortgage instead of rent," she said absently. "When you evaluate finances for a living, it's galling to spend money each month with nothing long-term to show for it. But the location of my apartment was so great for where I worked and there were no housing opportunities that felt right for me the last time I looked."

"We'll probably have to move farther out," Robert agreed, "but at least we'll be able to carpool."

"Such togetherness," Gwen commented. "Everett and I were so busy with our jobs and separate hobbies that we always had our own little lives. It was an adjustment when we both retired and started traveling even more. All this time to spend with each other!"

"But she means a good adjustment." Everett grinned at his wife.

Neely fidgeted in her chair. Marriage *was* an adjustment, she knew that. But she hadn't lived with another human being since college, which felt like a lifetime ago. What would Robert be like as a roommate? A *husband*, she reminded herself.

While there were a few shows she watched regularly, she often liked to unwind after work with a good book; Robert was a fan of television, whether he could find anything worth viewing or not. During their time at his apartment, she'd observed that he was perfectly content to flip through channels. Repeatedly.

He claimed he sometimes liked TV simply for the "background noise," but the concept of deliberately seeking out noise was foreign to her. Perhaps because she'd grown up with siblings, including Douglas, who'd been a loud, cheerfully obnoxious boy and Savannah, who'd always seemed to have giggling friends over, Neely appreciated peace and quiet.

Booo-ring. She could almost hear Vi's assessment.

Would Robert find her dull a year from now? *Stop panicking. He's known you for three years and is not under*

the delusion that you're a party animal. And surely she
wasn't so unforgivably rigid that the television in the
next room would bother her while she was reading.

Once they'd finished lunch, Gwen shot her
husband an apprehensive glance. "Dear, perhaps this
isn't the best time…."

"Perhaps not," Everett agreed.

Robert looked between his parents. "Is there a problem?"

"Not at all," Gwen assured him. "It's just that
before this latest jaunt, we saw our attorney and had
some, er, details updated. We aren't getting any
younger, you know. Your father was going to discuss
the paperwork with you after lunch, but in light of
your happy news—"

"It's not a problem," Robert assured his mother. "Why
don't I go with Dad, and you can keep Neely company?"

Neely would never have considered leaving Robert
alone with her mother during their first meeting, but
Gwen Walsh seemed unlikely to pounce and interro-
gate. She'd listened to them discuss houses without
once reaching for the real estate section of the Sunday
paper or offering her decision on what sort of floor
plan would be most advantageous. *I think I love these
people.* Maybe not their taste in timepieces, but definitely the people themselves.

Gwen smiled at Neely. "Since you liked those castle pictures, maybe you'd enjoy looking at some scrapbooks I've put together of Everett's and my travels?"

"Yes, thank you."

The afternoon passed pleasantly, with Gwen simply showing friendly interest in Neely. There were no siblings ragging anyone with outrageous remarks or threats to show unflattering baby pictures. Maybe this was why Robert had turned out to be such a great guy—lack of a large family driving him crazy and imbuing him with antisocial tendencies.

"They're like you," Neely said as Robert backed the car out of the driveway. "Wonderful!"

His smile was affectionate. "Glad you liked them."

"How could I not? Your mother was charming to talk to while you were with your dad, told me all kinds of stories about their travels."

"Yeah, they've always been busy and decided there was no reason retirement should be boring. Maybe next time they go somewhere, they'll bring you back a clock, too."

She changed the subject. "Everything's okay, right? With your folks? Your mom made it sound like they needed you to look over something serious."

"Standard paperwork on certain medical decisions

and their assets. They mention these things to me from time to time since I'm the only heir."

Neely knew that, in her family, Douglas and Savannah were the ones who had all the information about…their parents' final wishes. It occurred to her that, should anything happen to Gerald or Beth, she had her siblings to help her with any arrangements. Casting a glance at Robert, she thought perhaps she shouldn't have been so glib when he mentioned being an only child earlier. There must be times when that was difficult.

But the reminder that he stood to inherit whatever his parents left him, in addition to the nest eggs he and Neely had separately accumulated, made her think again about Leah's and Douglas's advice. She should ask Robert about a prenuptial agreement. It wasn't just two divorced people who suggested it; she'd recently been reading an article about prenups in a modern women's money magazine. She wished now that she'd left it lying around her apartment so that Robert could "accidentally" see it, thus sparking the discussion. Of course, she rarely left anything lying around and had put the periodical in the recycle bin when she'd finished with it.

"Hey," Robert said gently. "My parents are fine, this was just routine stuff. No reason for you to worry."

"Right." Since he thought she was concerned over his father's health, it seemed callous to admit she'd been thinking about financial matters. "They took the engagement news awfully well. Not that my family was upset, merely surprised. You must have really talked me up at Christmas."

"My parents tend to be mellow about my decisions, letting me live my own life."

"Must be nice to have that kind of unconditional support." Beth had originally contested that accounting was not a very feminine career. Luckily, Savannah was feminine enough for all of them. Once Vi hit her turbulent teen years, Beth was much slower to criticize anything Neely did.

At the moment, Neely wished she were a little more like Savannah. Though conversations with the opposite sex had never been Neely's forte, she knew there were things she needed to discuss with her soon-to-be husband. Having her sister's knack for gentle diplomacy would be pretty handy right now.

"Robert? Thinking of those legal worst-case documents…you're familiar with prenuptial agreements?"

His gaze knifed toward her. "I know what they are, obviously. I've never sat down and read one in my spare time."

"Well, no. Me neither. But I was thinking, maybe

it wouldn't be a bad idea. T-to get more familiar with them."

"Are you saying you *want* a prenup?"

"I'm saying maybe it's something we could explore."

"Why? We'd only need one if we got divorced." His guarded tone had become colder. "That's not how you see us ending up, is it?"

"Of course not." Damn it, she'd known she wouldn't be very good at this. "But if you approach it rationally, no one gets married thinking they're going to end up divorced. Leah was completely blindsided and, trust me, she wishes now that there'd been a prenup."

"Leah's husband was an ass who couldn't keep his hands off a twenty-year-old floozy! I would never do anything like that."

"Er, no. It was just an example." A bad one, Neely decided, biting her lip. Maybe she should have mentioned Douglas instead. He and his wife had parted more because of differences than clear fault. Or maybe she should stay away from concrete examples and stick to general terms. "The way I see it, prenups are analogous to death and dismemberment clauses. You hope you never need the protection when you sign it, but if you ever do—"

"Everyone dies, it's only a question of when. Not everyone gets divorced."

Not everyone gets dismembered, either, but people still take the insurance. She'd known that Robert, who chose to see the best in people and the humor in the world, would not jump for joy at this arguably cynical safety measure, but she was growing frustrated with his inability to even consider it.

"Look, Robert, I've had lots of postdivorce conversations with Leah that I could barely understand because she was crying so hard. And even though he didn't cry, my brother went through hell when Zoe left." She couldn't begin to imagine the gaping hole she'd have to cope with if she and Robert ever parted ways. Just because she wasn't as good as he was at expressing emotions didn't mean they weren't there. "If anything could have been done for either of them to make those ordeals even a tiny bit easier…"

Robert was silent for a long time, but she couldn't think of any arguments that were any stronger than the ones she'd already made. She could be patient. They still had a little while until they reached her apartment. Besides, she understood the value of thinking decisions over and appreciated that he hadn't just snapped back a retort.

"Maybe I don't believe divorce should be easy," he finally said. "Marriage is a very serious commitment, so why should it come with a built-in escape hatch?"

Well, hell, what was she supposed to say to that? That there may come a day when she was making him so crazy he'd be desperate for that escape?

He sighed. "Is this a deal-breaker?"

"What? No." Did he honestly think she'd call off their wedding over this? She happened to feel a pre-nuptial agreement was a sensible idea, but she wasn't about to blackmail him into one! He should know she wasn't going to bail just because they were having their first real argument. "I would remember if I'd answered your proposal with, 'Yes, Robert, I'd love to be your wife…as long as you sign here, here and here. And initial that last line there.'"

Unexpectedly, he laughed, sounding more himself. The invisible weight pressing against her chest lightened considerably.

"Then we'll talk to someone about it," he relented, meeting her halfway. "I'm not in favor of having one drawn up, but since I don't plan to ever use the damn thing anyway, what's it going to hurt to humor you?"

She scowled at the humoring part, but decided to be a gracious victor. "Thank you."

A moment later he flashed her a tenuous smile that was probably meant to signify they were okay again. Unfortunately, it didn't quite reach the mark.

The good news was, they'd survived the disagreement. She supposed the romantic thing to do now would be to kiss and make up, but since he was behind the wheel of a car, she simply tried to move the conversation to more upbeat ground.

"Your parents made me realize I've never been that many places." She liked being in control of her environment, sticking to a routine. Waking up in lots of strange hotels hadn't been something she craved, but after seeing those pictures today, she could easily envision how visiting beautiful places with someone you loved could be magical. Maybe she'd never been bit by the travel bug because she hadn't had anyone with whom to share special locations. "Did you go with them a lot when you were younger?"

"Some. Other times they left me with my uncle, so I could play with my cousins and they could have quality time alone. They got more active with their jaunts after I left home."

"Do you think we'll go lots of fabulous places together?" She wanted to hit home that she was planning to be with him for a long, long time to come.

But his tone was still uncharacteristically flat. "Maybe. We certainly won't have any kids restricting our travel. And it's not like we'll need to save up for college tuitions."

At the wistful note in his tone, alarm edged through her. "Did you want kids?"

"No. I mean, once upon a time, I thought about having a family of my own. But...I have you now. That's enough."

No pressure.

She should have just let it alone—the prenup mention alone had left her feeling as if she were strolling through a conversational minefield—but she was in a truly committed relationship now. She had to learn how to have these personal, if difficult, discussions. And shouldn't she get to know him as well as possible before they vowed to join their lives together forever? "So, you and I won't have kids, but if you'd married younger, you might have wanted them?"

"I thought you were too pragmatic for 'what ifs.'"

But *he* wasn't. He was a man with a lot of love to give, one who would have made a great father. In contrast, Neely wasn't sure she had the maternal gene. The first infant she'd ever cared for was Vi, whom she'd babysat frequently; the experiences had not left her hankering to change diapers or warm bottles at two in the morning.

If she'd married years ago and had a child, she was sure she would have loved it, but now she was set in her ways. Happy with her habits and spotless apartment. Watching her nephews, Trent and Adam, achieve their milestones and grow into fine young men had been very rewarding and fulfilled any parental urges she might have had. Robert, on the other hand, was an only child and had never even enjoyed that vicarious experience. Would losing his chance to be a father taint their marriage?

She'd thought of Leah several times today, recalling how hard her divorce had hit her. Now Neely thought of the new young bride who would be replacing her friend. Men could reproduce much later in life than women. Hadn't she read somewhere once that Charlie Chaplin had still fathered children into his seventies?

"I can't really see myself as a mother, especially this late in my life," she said candidly. "I know women have done it before, but... If, hypothetically, you'd fallen for a younger woman, would you go ahead and try to have children?"

"Are you, hypothetically, asking if I might regret down the road not marrying someone else?" The sarcasm in his tone was unlike him.

"No!" An uncharacteristic blush heated her face.

"I suppose if I do decide to run off for a younger woman with lots of eggs left, that prenup will come in handy," he snapped.

Oh, I give up! She'd witnessed enough bickering in

her family to have a sense of when a conversation was just not going to be productive. Like now. Clearly, he was still upset about earlier. Any meaningful discussion would have to wait for a time when they were calmer—*they* meaning *him*.

CHAPTER 8

Savannah stood at the kitchen sink, rinsing plates and finding a sort of numbing comfort in the familiar chore. Though she was excited for Trent and had smiled over his enthusiasm at the dinner table, his plans to spend spring break next month with a former classmate on the UNC campus left her with mixed emotions. Footsteps fell behind her, heavier and slower than her teenage son's normal dash through the room to grab a cola.

Jason. As her husband moved closer, her stomach fluttered in a way that brought on pleasant déjà vu. He smelled good, the warm spice of his cologne enveloping her, reminding her how excited she used to get when he pulled her into his arms at the end of the date, the way she'd breathe in the scent of his aftershave just before he'd kiss the breath right out of her.

Her heart beat in an old, familiar erratic rhythm as

he stopped behind her. Perhaps because she'd reminisced yesterday about her newlywed days, her body was now responding with a giddy eagerness she hadn't experienced recently. Trent was at the other end of the house, and she was alone with her husband in a way that had become rare over the last few hectic years. Jason's body brushed hers slightly as he leaned in— and opened the cabinet just over her shoulder.

He withdrew a tumbler and turned toward the refrigerator. "The chicken tonight was great, babe."

"Thank you."

The motor of the ice dispenser whirred and cubes *clunk, clunk, clunked* into his waiting glass, each seeming to land in the pit of her stomach. Idiot, she told herself as Jason left the room. She didn't think she was foolish for the bright, unexpectedly sharp pull of desire she'd experienced; there was nothing wrong with wanting your husband. But the tears pricking her eyes seemed silly. It wasn't as if he was some unrequited teen crush. They were married. If she wanted to be close, she could always go join him on the couch, cuddle up to him as he watched the news.

Or *he* could cuddle up to *me*, a stubborn voice whined inside her head. She hated that voice. It sounded so…petulant. But it was also persistent, refusing to be ignored. *Has he touched you at all since he got home from golf today?* Had he kissed her hello before he hopped in the shower? Had he pulled out her chair at dinner, the way he used to? Had his hand brushed over hers as they sat listening to Trent planning his upcoming visit to the campus for a taste of college life?

No.

Savannah could list at least a dozen opportunities for her husband to touch her this evening, and he'd taken none of them. And to think she'd bragged yesterday to her sisters about a time when she and Jason couldn't get enough of each other.

Recalling her sisters, she stiffened her spine. Somehow, she couldn't imagine Vi moping in the kitchen over an inattentive date. Vi would probably march into the living room, switch off the television set and throw her man down on the couch. After mulling over that brazen option for three uncomfortable nanoseconds, Savannah comforted herself with the reminder that, at the other end of the house or not, Trent *was* still here. Any throwing down should probably take place behind a closed bedroom door. Maybe she could dig that silky sky-blue nightshirt with the low neckline out of the back of the closet tonight and give Jason a good-night kiss that didn't send him off to slumber land.

Her heart pounded approval of this plan. Why *not* seduce her husband? Maybe the blue funk she'd been trying to ignore lately was part sexual frustration. She shut the dishwasher and checked the clock above the stove. As much as she was suddenly looking forward to bedtime, it was only seven-thirty. Might as well get some laundry done while she was waiting for bedtime.

Padding down the hall, she smiled to herself as she passed the living room and heard the muffled sounds of whatever Jason was watching now. Warm memories of previous encounters tempted her to go kiss him, but mischievous anticipation was part of the enjoyment. Just as it had been when she was in college, spending an entire Saturday looking forward to the moment he picked her up at her dorm. With a happy sigh, she absently sorted clothes in the laundry room and tossed a small load of darks into the washer.

Before she started the machine, however, she decided she should check with her son. Savannah had always tried to keep a clean, well-run house, but once Adam had left, she'd accepted that her boys had to learn to do for themselves. She'd adopted the policy that Trent was responsible for keeping his own room neat with no assistance or nagging from her. Unfortunately, they had very different views of acceptable living conditions, so it was best for everyone if she just avoided his room whenever possible. Now would be a good time for an exception, though. Why run a load that wasn't really full when he probably had jeans stowed in his room that were capable of walking around on their own?

Armed with an empty white laundry basket for dirty clothes she didn't plan to touch any longer than possible, she retraced her steps up the hall. Rock music spilled out through the partially open door of Trent's room. It wasn't cranked to its usual decibel, however, and when she heard his voice, she figured he was on the phone with his girlfriend. Savannah had to admit she was relieved the two teenagers would be going to different colleges come fall. She didn't mind if they ended up together, she just wanted them to consider other options before they got any more serious. They were both good kids, but *kids*, in Savannah's opinion, was still the operative word.

"…want you to get the full experience, we just want you to be smart, too."

Savannah drew up short—that deep voice wasn't Trent's, but his father's. She'd assumed Jason was in the living room.

"Don't worry, Dad." Trent's tone was laced with good-natured impatience. "I know there are parties on campus, but it'll be a lot tamer than if I went with my friends to some beach down in Florida for spring break."

As if Savannah would have allowed such a thing!

"If I did have anything to drink—and I'm not saying I will—I can just walk back to where I'm staying, so you don't have to worry about me driving at all. And between a dad who delivers babies for a living *and* a big brother, I've got the condom lecture so many times I could practically teach sex-ed."

The laundry hamper slipped from Savannah's grip, but didn't make much noise against the soft carpeting. It wasn't as if she naively believed Trent ended his dates with a cordial handshake, but it was still jarring to hear her baby talk about condoms and sex. Lord, she hoped he was speaking in the hypothetical. *When did he grow up?* She glanced at the pristine stretch of white wall, where the crayon graffiti had been painted over years ago. Was it an optical illusion that she swore she could see its faint outline?

Her son so matter-of-factly discussing a love life had a dampening effect on her own plans for the night. What had she said to Neely and Vi? *"We aren't twenty anymore."* Good God. *She.* wasn't twenty, but Trent would be before she knew it. Adam already was. Suddenly, her question wasn't when had the boys become men, but when had she turned into her mother? A middle-aged woman who'd soon have grown children all gone from the house.

I don't feel middle-aged. At least, she hadn't back in the kitchen when her husband stood close to her and sexual awareness had gripped her. But they acted on those impulses less and less. Jason barely gave any sign of feeling them. Were their best days already behind them, those newlywed moments of talking until sunrise without even meaning to, being excited to see each other at the end of the day or reaching for each other right after sex because even though they were both satisfied, they still needed to touch?

If all that was past, what was her future?

"Will you let Mom know you talked to me and that I'm not going to do anything stupid while I'm gone next month?" Trent asked his dad. "She looked a little freaked at dinner."

"She loves you," Jason said. "It's normal that she worries about you. And cut her a little slack if she's…clingier than usual. Women her age go through a lot. You and your brother leaving are a major part of that, but she's also got her own issues to deal with."

"Ugh. If you mean stuff like hormones, I don't want to hear about it."

His father laughed and said something else, but Savannah was already fleeing in the opposite direction. Her mother had always said you shouldn't eavesdrop because you might hear something you don't like. How true.

Jason's voice rang in her ears. *Women her age?* Maybe he hadn't looked in the mirror lately, but he was no younger than she was! To have her child and her husband discuss her like that, as if she were a quirky older relative to be indulged, burned a trail of stinging humiliation through her.

She wished she could turn back the clock a few minutes and say the hell with Trent's jeans, he could do his own laundry. But if she could reverse time, why stop there? She wished she could go years back to when she was young and fresh, with her boys close and her whole life ahead of her. Since she couldn't, slipping into her coziest flannel pajamas and trying to lose herself in a good book sounded like a decent alternative. Flannel wouldn't arouse her husband, but so what? She'd already removed seduction from the itinerary.

After all, she wouldn't want Jason to think she was clinging.

Compartmentalizing emotions was more difficult when you were in love. Still, Neely thought she was doing an admirable job. All day Monday, she'd been busy with strategic meetings and had managed to offer valuable input. She doubted any of her colleagues knew how preoccupied she was with Robert. They'd parted on strained terms when he dropped her off yesterday and knowing he was here in the building, made it difficult to focus on work. But she managed reasonably well, up until the time she bumped into him right outside her office.

"I was hoping to catch you." He smiled, the expression both wan and tender, and all of the emotions she'd been fighting rushed to the forefront in a surge that broadsided her like a breaking wave.

"Hi." The word was a choked effort. Perhaps she'd be less on edge if she'd managed to sleep last night, but she'd tossed and turned, thinking that, for once, the solitude felt an awful lot like big, empty loneliness. "D-do you want to come into my office to talk?"

He nodded. "I know you must have a lot to do before you can leave this evening, but…" It wasn't until they were alone with the door shut that he finished his thought. "I was miserable last night."

She felt a rush of joy at his words—and a guilty sort of relief that he'd admitted it first. "Me, too."

"I shouldn't have been so caustic with you. I guess it's like you always say." He leaned against her desk, glancing at her hands as if he were considering reaching for them. "Families make you crazy."

"But yours is so normal," she said with a laugh. "No

suggestion that we call ourselves the Walsons, no wheeling out every embarrassing photo you—"

"Neely, did you even see a photo of me? The marker of where the Berlin wall used to be, sure. The Wallace Monument in Scotland, absolutely."

Now that she thought about it, she didn't recall a lot of family pictures.

"It's not like I'm complaining," he said gently. "At my age, it would be a little silly to still have my high school mug shot sitting on the mantel. I'm just trying to illustrate a point. My parents are good people, but I grew up feeling somewhat…detached. I think in my youth I might have interpreted their particular child-raising philosophy as indifference. I became determined to express my own emotions, to be in very affectionate relationships."

Well, that explained a lot about Robert's disposition. On the other hand, it raised questions about what he could possibly see in her.

Instead of voicing her insecurities, she said lightly, "A man who's actually comfortable with his feelings— I can't believe another woman didn't snap you up years ago."

He shifted uncomfortably. "Some of my past relationships, especially in my twenties, I might have come on a little, er, strong. Women who broke up with me didn't specifically use the words *stalker* or *codependent,* but I was not the mellow man you see before you today. Unfortunately, a few bouts with rejection made me try even harder, which as you can imagine, was the wrong way to go."

Even though she knew Robert well enough to know he'd recovered from past heartbreaks, she flinched for the earnest, eager-to-love young man he must have been. She wanted to pull him close to her and wrap him in the assurance that his heart was safe now.

"Those women were shortsighted, and their loss was definitely my gain," she said.

"Thank you. All that talk yesterday about prenups and divorce pricked my male ego. I don't like to think of myself as still having those old vulnerabilities, but it can be…unsettling at times, to think maybe you're not as invested in this relationship as I am."

Her warm, fuzzy feelings toward him took a sharp left turn. "How can you say that?" He was the only man she'd ever seriously considered a long-term future with; they were planning a wedding for God's sake! She'd canceled some important work tomorrow so that she could spend even more time with her family—something that seemed to have quadrupled since Robert popped the question—and hunt for a dress that would in all probability make her look like a walking doily.

Shortly thereafter, she'd be hunting for a house, taking the scary step of actually moving in with someone else and merging her life with his. A life she'd grown quite comfortable with these past few decades.

Maybe using endearments didn't come naturally to her and she was unlikely to cut pink construction paper to make homemade Valentine's Day cards, but didn't he see how much he meant to her? "They say actions speak louder than words, but if that were true, I don't know how you could question my feelings for you, Robert. The changes we're making, the sacrifices I'm willing—"

"Sacrifices?" He straightened, his posture tense.

"Maybe that was too strong a word." She bit her bottom lip. "But there are things I'll be giving up. L-like my apartment."

His eyes hardened, boring into hers. "*This* is what I mean by not as invested. I'll be giving up my place, too, remember? But I don't look at it as a sacrifice, Neely. I see it as a beginning, something I'm looking forward to. I hope I'm not the only one."

By virtue of them working together, he easily scored the last word. He left her office before she could figure out how to rebut. And chasing him past the copy machine so she could explain that wasn't what she'd meant didn't seem very professional.

So she sank into her chair, instead.

What was going on here? In the entire time she and Robert dated, they'd barely ever fought. Now even their *apologizing* had deteriorated into a disagreement. It had been weeks since she'd felt her normal calm, cool, collected self. Weren't weddings supposed to be happy events?

Did planning one stress everyone out this much, or was she somehow nuptially deficient? If she was feeling really brave, she could ask her sisters tomorrow. Few people were as delighted to point out your flaws as your siblings.

Irony being what it was, it just figured that Neely found such a flattering dress on a day she and Robert had argued. She stared into the wide three-paneled mirror, studying the woman in a simple off-shoulder cream gown with an A-line-style skirt and a tiny bit of midsection beading that gave the illusion of a better defined waist. The bride-to-be reflected was surprisingly lovely. Or would be if she smiled.

"Well. I suppose this one is it," she said to the women standing behind her.

"Yes," Savannah agreed listlessly. "You look great."

Vi shrugged. "I can't tell much difference between that one and the others, but it doesn't make your butt look bad and you have nice shoulders, so I say go for it."

With their outpouring of enthusiasm, they might as well have been the Wedding Party of the Damned. Maybe Neely should ask the salesperson—who'd gone up front to answer the phone—if there were any bridesmaid's dresses available in black. Vi would be thrilled.

"Are you sure you guys like it?" she prodded. "You don't sound very…upbeat."

"Please." Vi lifted a brow. "Like you've been a living portrait of joy today? And *you're* the one getting married."

"Yeah." Neely heaved a sigh.

Savannah approached, her expression softening. "Neely, darlin', you're not getting cold feet are you? It's normal to be nervous, but Robert loves you."

"We've had a couple of…differences of opinion lately," Neely admitted. "I met his parents this weekend."

"It didn't go well?" her older sister asked.

"No, it went great. They're lovely. At least, I think so. I get the impression Robert would have liked them to be a bit more demonstrative—that he'd like *me* to be. His mom happened to mention something about their will and on the way home, I was thinking about legal precautions and how Douglas offered to recommend someone to help with a prenuptial agreement. So I asked Robert if maybe we should have one."

"Oh, Neely." This from Vi in an exasperated what-is-the-matter-with-you tone. The young woman probably wouldn't appreciate being told she sounded a lot like their mother just then. "You told Robert you wanted a prenup?"

"What's wrong with that?" Savannah wanted to know. "I happen to think it's a very sensible decision."

Neely blinked, surprised Little Ms. Empowerment was chiding her while the domestic goddess of home and hearth acknowledged divorce as a possibility.

"Sensible? It's a betrayal of their love!" Vi's melodramatic air was a living flashback to her teen years.

"Vidalia Jean, of the three of us I'm the only one here who's actually married, so you listen to me. Love is the necessary foundation, but marriage is complicated. It's mortgages and hard decisions and slogging through day-to-day habits without making each other too nuts. Half the couples Jason and I have known over the years have split up. Numbers and risk management are part of Neely's life. Do you really think she should be oblivious to the statistics, that she should ignore even the *possibility?*"

"Yes!" Vi was strangely vehement about this for someone who'd never sustained a romantic relationship. "Women don't need a big, strong husband to take care of them. Neely can pay her own bills, and she could certainly go out and find sex without changing her name to do it. People live together all the time these days without a marriage license. She already has good health insurance and U.S. citizenship. So, what's the point of going through all this trouble except love, the honest belief that she and Robert will be together forever? Why do it half-assed?"

"That's rich coming from you," Neely snapped. She was in no mood to be lectured on commitment from her aimless little sister. "Or, maybe it's not. You know a lot about going through life half-assed."

"And you're so up on *my* life because of those regular sisterly chats we have?" Vi demanded. "Wait, I forgot you were the one who's so detached she pretends her family doesn't exist except for one Sunday a month."

"That's not true!"

"Isn't it? I helped Douglas move into his apartment, but I don't remember seeing you there. Have you even been to see his new place? Savannah might irritate the hell out of him with her perky drop-ins to have lunch downtown—"

"Hey! Douglas doesn't say I irritate him."

"—but at least she worried about him after the divorce."

"I worry about him," Neely said softly, her tone a sharp contrast to their previously raised voices. "Just because I'm not…the most touchy-feely person on the planet, that doesn't mean I don't care." Why did no one understand that?

Ever the family diplomat, Savannah came to the rescue, placing her hand on Vi's shoulder. "Neely was as upset about his divorce as the rest of us, but his situation only highlights the reasons why signing a prenup might be a good idea."

A heavy silence fell over them, and Neely felt like the world's biggest hypocrite standing there in the gorgeous wedding dress that should have been a symbol of hope, faith and an unrelenting optimism about love. She certainly hoped she had it in her to be a good *wife* because, so far, she was lousy bride material.

CHAPTER 9

The better-known expression might be "guilt money," but in the South, there was also guilt food. Another woman, for instance, one with actual culinary skills, might bake something to show Robert she was sorry for their argument. While Neely couldn't fall back on cooking to make up for the argument with Vi, she at least had a charge card she knew how to use.

"Can I buy you two dinner?" Neely asked as they climbed into her car.

They'd left the dress boutique with orders for the saleswoman to hold Neely's gown. She was almost positive it was the dress she would buy—and not just because she couldn't stand any more shopping—but she wanted to think it over and bring Leah this weekend for a final opinion. Possibly Beth, as well. Meanwhile, they could start discussing styles for the bride's attendants.

"Sounds good to me," Savannah said dully. "Jason's at the hospital tonight, and Trent said he was going to Steve's to study for their physics exam."

"As long as I can still get home in the next few hours. I'm doing a late shift at the club tonight." Vi's mutinous expression was reflected in the rearview mirror. "Is this because you feel bad that the shopping expedition we tried to help you with turned into a shouting match?"

"Maybe a little. Does that mean you don't want to go?"

"Hell, no." Vi grinned suddenly. "It means I should order something really expensive to help absolve you of your guilt."

Despite the obnoxious statement, Neely grinned back. Her sister was bizarrely likable when she wasn't annoying the shit out of you.

"Is it really necessary to swear so often?" Savannah asked.

Good thing she couldn't read minds, Neely thought guiltily.

"You're an intelligent young woman, Vidalia. I know you could express yourself equally well without vulgarity."

"Doubtful, but thanks for saying I'm smart. I always suspected I was the brains in the family."

Savannah snorted. Well, sniffed loudly, but close enough.

Neely turned to her older sister. "Is she wearing her seat belt? If not, I could take a sharp turn and she might fall out."

They heard the distinctive *snick* of Vi locking her door. Just in case.

A few moments later, however, Vi had announced she'd be willing to jump from the moving vehicle the next time they passed a restaurant that wasn't already packed. Looked as if they weren't the only people in the area ready to eat dinner. Finally, Neely spotted a place with a comparatively empty lot.

"What about this one?" she asked.

"Kind of makes you wonder how good they are to be doing such a slow business," Savannah remarked. "But at least I don't have to cook."

"I'm not choosy," Vi said, already getting out of the car before Neely had pulled the keys from the ignition.

Inside, they were seated in the back corner. It was one of those generic restaurants whose decor and menu was identical to about half a dozen other franchises. A bored-looking waitress plunked down three ice waters—minus lemon wedges or straws—before disappearing to flirt with two cute guys who had just snagged a booth.

"Doesn't she know they're probably gay?" Vi asked, rolling her eyes. "It would serve her right if we left her section. We could sit at the bar and tip heavily. Maybe flirt for free drinks."

Savannah laughed. "With my sex appeal, I'd be lucky to get a free glass of ice."

"Are you kidding? You've kept yourself in great shape," Vi argued. "I want a body like yours when I'm your age."

"My age," Savannah echoed dryly. "According to the men I live with, I've hit a delicate life stage and should be handled with kid gloves. Not that my husband bothers handling me at all these days."

Damn. Neely had hoped that the melancholy she'd sensed in her sister the other day was an aberration, hoped she'd misheard Savannah's comment about marriage in the dress shop. Studying the defeated slump of her sister's shoulders, Neely recalled the way Savannah had championed the prenup decision. The thought of Savannah and Jason splitting up made her gut clench.

Vi's wrong. I do care. But caring didn't always give her insight on how to help.

After a moment of silence to ponder the situation, Vi caught Neely's gaze. "I say we get her blotto."

"You mean inebriated?" Savannah arched one

eyebrow in a haughty expression. "I do not drink in excess."

"Yeah, there's a lot of things you don't seem to do," Vi muttered.

Savannah fisted her hands on the tabletop. "Give her a few degrees and she thinks she has all the answers. Tell me, what good would getting drunk do? In the morning, I'd be left with a hangover, fewer brain cells and the exact same damn problems."

Vi blinked. "Did she just say damn?"

"Guess swearing is one of the things she does do," Neely said with a grin. Angry was better than defeated in her opinion.

"No, I don't! Vulgarity is even more pointless than drinking. Everyone knows you can catch more flies with honey than vinegar."

"I say we put your honey theory to the test and send you to the bar for drinks," Vi cajoled.

"I am a married woman, and I have dignity. I will not bat my eyelashes at some boy young enough to be my son to get you a discounted beer."

"I'm sorry, d'you say you wanted beer?" The negligent waitress stopped at their table, pencil hovering over her notepad.

Vi nodded before Savannah could correct the woman. "We'll take a pitcher."

After they decided on a brand, Savannah shook her head. "You can order it, but that doesn't mean I'm drinking it."

"More for me," Vi said cheerfully. "If I end up like cousin Phoebe, it's all your fault."

Phoebe was Aunt Josephine and Uncle Darnell's daughter. In Neely's opinion, her thirty-six-year-old cousin was not an alcoholic. Just the family lush. She could go long stretches at a time without drinking or giving any indication of even thinking about it, but when alcohol was around, she didn't know when to stop and generally made a fool of herself and whatever relatives were in the vicinity. If the family could get beer banned from the annual reunions and Uncle Vernon to stop spiking the holiday punch at Christmas, there would be significantly fewer cringeworthy photos each year.

By the time the waitress returned with the ordered pitcher and empty glasses, they'd all decided on dinner selections. Vi filled three cups, but Neely figured Savannah's would go untouched. Neely, on the other hand, had been in a crappy mood for the past couple of days and was more than happy to accept a drink. She had no plans to be the next Phoebe, but there were worse things than a cold, commiserative beer with your sisters when you and your lover weren't getting along.

Huh. It stopped her midsip, to realize how companionable this outing had become. When was the last time she'd planned to do something with her sisters just for the hell of it? If it weren't for the wedding dress search, which was thankfully coming to a close, she never would have thought to call Vi or Savannah and tell them about the prenup disagreement. Leah, certainly, or possibly even Amanda from work. But not her sisters.

"Thank you, guys, for your help," she said. "With all this wedding stuff."

"We're just getting started," Savannah reminded her, brightening. "You've got to think about flowers, invitations, music, the reception—"

"Marital attorneys," Vi muttered.

"Watch it," Neely warned. "I was just starting to think you weren't a complete brat."

Vi smiled winningly. "Oh, I am. Now that we've got that established, can I go back to making smart-ass comments?"

"When did you *stop?*" Savannah wanted to know, causing them all to laugh.

Throughout dinner—which was bland and over-cooked, made more edible by the second round of beer—they worked on the list Savannah and Beth had made the night Neely announced her engagement.

"I hope I haven't forgotten anything," Savannah said, although Neely couldn't imagine what more could possibly go into a wedding. "Too bad Mama's not here."

"That's a matter of opinion," Vi muttered into her cup.

Savannah bristled. "I think she's earned a little more respect than that, Vidalia."

"Of course *you* do."

"What is that supposed to mean?"

"Just that not all of us have the same nifty relationship with her that you always have," Vi said, her words more matter-of-fact than accusatory. "You can do no wrong."

"Well, I hate to criticize, Vi, but most of the trouble you've ever been in with our parents has been your own doing."

"Some of it." Vi shrugged. "But it's more than that. You understand what I'm talking about, don't you, Neely?"

Damn it. This was a conversation Neely had managed to dodge for over forty years—was it really necessary to have it now?

"Neely?" Savannah prompted, hurt replacing her earlier smile.

"Our mother loves us each in our own way," Neely said. "Even you, Vi. But you have to admit, Savannah, you and Mom have always been particularly close."

"It's not as if I've ever tried to exclude the two of you! You just had different interests. For years, Mama dropped me off and picked me up from ballet lessons. I helped her peel vegetables for dinner, and we chatted in the kitchen. She helped me with my homework, helped me put on makeup for school dances. Neely, as I recall, you scoffed at both school dances and ballet, and, Vi, I doubt you ever needed tutoring. You've always been freakishly smart when you weren't ditching class. I guess, I was never as independent as the two of you."

From Vi's expression, Neely could see the admiration in Savannah's voice was a shock to them both.

"I never thought of it that way," Vi admitted.

When the moment of silence lingered, Neely thought perhaps they should return to wedding details rather than childhood. "This list was very helpful, Savannah, thanks. But I want to run some of this by Leah, too. My maid of honor should be in on the plans."

"Especially for the bachelorette party," Vi said, gesturing with her fork. "Can it be really dirty?"

"No." Neely laughed, then turned to Savannah. "Is it just me, or does she think about sex a lot?"

"So I like sex. Don't you?" Vi challenged.

"Well…sure," Neely answered, a blush climbing her cheeks as she thought about Robert. They hadn't spent the night with each other in almost a week, and she was starting to really feel his absence. The fact that wanting him left her so flustered was ludicrous. She was hardly a teenager thinking her first lusty thoughts.

"And you have make-up sex to look forward to!" Vi said enthusiastically.

Savannah bobbed her head, her gaze warm. "Jason and I don't fight much, but there have been one or two doozies over the years. And the making up afterward… Lordy."

"This is actually Robert's and my first fight—although *fight* may be too strong a word." She recalled the angry look he'd hurled at her when she'd said she was sacrificing for their relationship. "Or maybe not."

"The best way to put it behind you," Vi advised, "is to go to his place and jump his bones."

"So you're my relationship guru now?" Neely asked affectionately.

Vi wrinkled her nose. "I'm not sure I qualify as much of a relationship expert, but I *have* jumped my share of men."

Clearly uncomfortable, Savannah squirmed in her seat. It was one thing to know Vi had an active sex life, another for their younger sister to talk so openly about a string of lovers, especially when Savannah herself had been with only one man.

"Here, let me pour you some more," Neely said quickly, trying to head off any criticism.

Though she didn't subscribe to their mother's cow-and-free-milk theory, Neely also found it hard to approve of Vi's casual attitude toward sex. Still, after shouting at Vi in the boutique about her "half-assed" life earlier, there had probably been enough disapproval expressed for one evening.

Savannah barely acknowledged the draft refill. "Vi, promise me you're being really, really careful. And I don't just mean, be *careful* who you go home with because he could be a chainsaw-wielding psycho, but be careful. Condoms break, hasty decisions can be less pleasant in the morning—"

"I'm a big girl, Savannah. And I'm happy with my choices."

"Are you?" To her credit, Savannah didn't sound judgmental, merely curious. "Happy, I mean?"

Vi glanced at her plate. "Who's really happy all of the time?"

"Point taken," Savannah said quietly.

Suddenly Vi reached across the table, taking their older sister's hand. "Can we help? I know you and Jason love each other a lot, but you've admitted you're not getting everything you'd like out of your marriage. Do you want to talk about it? Do you want a makeover to put a little extra bounce in your step? Do you want us to help you make a voodoo doll in his image? I've got an artist friend in midtown who could probably put together a remarkable likeness."

Even though the offer wasn't aimed at her, Neely was genuinely touched by Vi's wish to make things better, especially since she realized that she wanted to assist just as badly.

"I don't know, but thank you for asking." Savannah sniffed, blinking to regain her composure. "I don't even know where I get off feeling so sorry for myself when there are hundreds of people out there with *real* problems. I have a nice home, a healthy family and a husband who's pretty great. I mean, no one's perfect every day, right? Hell, maybe it's just me and he's right about it being some damn 'life phase' making me crazy."

Vi and Neely exchanged glances, and Neely could see the worry her younger sister forced back in exchange for a teasing smile. *Funny, I never realized until now how much she looks like Douglas.* Something in the eyes, the set of the features. The spirit and good heart beneath the surface.

"I'll take your swearing twice in the same sentence as a positive omen," Vi joked.

Savannah raised her cup. "A positive omen, indeed. To good things just around the corner for all the Mason sisters!"

They clinked their glasses, tipped back their on-special beer and hoped for the best.

It was a full moon. Neely had almost reached the top of the stairs before she caught sight of the huge orb through the trees, so bright it was almost silver. Normally, she would have noticed the glowing night sky as she was driving, but she'd been busy chatting with her sisters. Once she'd dropped them off, her thoughts had been consumed with this.

"Promise me you'll do it," Vi had said, leaning her head back in the car for one last goodbye and a final bossy suggestion.

"Vi, my sex life is none of your business."

"No, but you're my sister, and I want you to be happy. Trust me on this, you should go to him."

"I promise to think it over," Neely had prevaricated. In all honesty, the decision had been made as they'd waited for the check. A couple had come in, young and smiling, choosing to sit on the same bench instead of across from each other in their booth. With the passion they'd radiated, Neely was surprised they hadn't glowed as brightly as tonight's moon. Looking at them had made her eager to get to Robert. Love wasn't just for the young.

Truthfully, her first experiences, back in college, had been awkward. In addition to feeling shy, she hadn't been able to shake the guilt that Beth Mason would *kill* her if she'd known what her daughter was doing at that moment. And things had ended so wretchedly with Daniel. She'd been suckered in by his "bad boy" appeal without realizing he was indeed a bad boy, quick to throw her aside when he was ready for a new challenge. She'd still been trying to cope with the breakup when she overheard him at a party, laughing about her sexual ineptitude with a drinking buddy.

For a long time after that, sex hadn't been something she looked forward to. In more recent relationships, it had been pleasant and she'd grown more confident in herself, but she'd also been able to compartmentalize her lovers, not dwell on them when she wasn't with them. Robert had crept into every area of her life.

Because he was such a demonstrative man, he was an incredible lover. Vi might tease Neely about her age, remind her that her breasts weren't getting any perkier with time, but Robert didn't care. He'd seen her naked for the first time a few months ago, and he'd seemed pretty damn happy with her. His appreciation helped her tap an inner, very female power, she realized as she reached his doorstep. Heady stuff that left her feeling sensual and, tonight, possessive. This man was hers. If she rarely knew how to tell him that, she could try to show him.

She'd arrived in a state of nearly euphoric longing, her courage bolstered by a few drinks and her sisters' encouragement. Now that she was actually knocking on the door, she wondered if he'd turned in for the night. It wasn't unthinkably late, but it was no longer early, either.

Except for his bare feet, Robert was fully dressed when he opened the door, the shirt he'd worn to work untucked and rolled up at the cuffs. His eyes grew round, registering shock when he saw her there. It never failed to surprise her, with all the neighbors he had frequently dropping by, that he didn't bother identifying visitors through the peephole first. But that was the man she loved, throwing his door open to anyone without reservation.

"Neely. Hi."

"You don't mind that I'm stopping in without calling first, do you?" She entered the apartment as she spoke, lifting up on her toes to press a quick kiss to his cheek. His body tightened even at that brief contact.

"Of course not. I want you to make yourself at home here. Until we find one of our own."

A thrill shot through her, earlier fears forgotten in tonight's boldness. "Let's start looking. Or at least call some real-estate agents this week, find one we like?"

The uncertainty in his gaze melted to a warmer welcome. "Sounds great. Is that why you came, to talk about this?"

"No." She stared at him with unmistakable determination. Once she'd cleared the air about a thing or two, she didn't plan for there to be much talking at all. "I found my wedding dress today."

"Oh."

"I'm looking forward to our wedding, Robert, to being your wife. You said sometimes you're not sure I'm as invested—"

"I'm sorry. It's not fair to project my insecurities on you."

She pressed two fingers against his mouth, leaving them there even after he'd stopped talking, lazily tracing the texture of his lips. "We're both entitled to our feelings, even when they differ. You aren't the only one who's wondered about the depth of my emotion. My own family wonders sometimes, and I don't blame any of you. There was a very brief time when I wore my heart on my sleeve and tried to live unrestrained and impulsive. It ended with me feeling like an ass, and I became even more restrained than before. I can't apologize for being who I am because that's the woman you fell in love with. But I did come here to show you what you mean to me, so you can think back to tonight whenever you wonder just how invested I am.

"Plus," she added with a half smile, "the way Vi explained it, you and I owe each other really hot make-up sex."

His breath hitched and steel fire blazed in his gray eyes. He stepped forward to take her in his arms, kissing her deeply. Thick desire flooded her veins, pooling inside her. That heady feeling she'd gloried in as she came to his door was multiplied a hundredfold. She'd never felt so *earthy* before, so inspired to just be completely natural with a man, unworried about holding anything back.

When the kiss broke, she pulled Robert's shirt off, running her fingers over his skin.

"Exactly what did this hot make-up sex entail?" he asked with an expectant smile.

She tugged his hand, leading him toward the bedroom. "I'll show you." That was, after all, the point. Letting him know with her actions how very much she loved him and wanted him to be a part of her.

CHAPTER 10

Vi stood at the bar, waiting for the bartender to stock her "bank." The man's name was Crash; he had a smooth, completely shaved head and kind eyes that seemed incongruous with his gladiator build. He tended bar on the slow nights and worked as a bouncer on weekends, splitting tips with the servers.

"Here ya go." He handed her the small money bag, now stocked with ones, fives and tens to make change, to strap around her waist. Crash grinned, raking an appreciative glance over her shirt.

It wasn't exactly low cut, but the strategically shaped neckline and the push-up bra beneath enhanced her cleavage. *Those of us not built like Neely gotta work with what we have.* The crimson shirt, matched to her lipstick, also bared her midriff, showing enough skin to offset relaxed jeans and thick-soled boots.

"You look great, but it seems kinda a waste for as few as we got in," he remarked. Tuesdays were notoriously slow nights, but it was her turn in the rotation. "Maybe you'll hit a big tipper, though."

She laughed. "I try to dress for myself, but a little help with textbooks for summer sessions would come in handy."

"More schoolin'? Leaves me in the dust, since I barely made it through high school. What are you going to do with all that fancy education?"

Since she had absolutely no idea, she answered, "You could pick up some classes if you wanted to. Not just college, but technical training, even informal continuing ed through community centers."

The big man shuddered. "I'll leave that stuff to you scholars and stick to pouring whiskey. Speaking of which…" With a final smile, he ambled toward the new customer who'd just settled herself on a bar stool.

Vi made a lazy pass through the room. On the weekends, there could be as many as four waitresses working, but for Monday through Wednesday, they usually got by with just a bartender and one waitress. Two if someone had rented the upstairs loft for a private party or meeting. Vi preferred working busy nights, not just for the tips but because she normally fed off the energy of the crowd. Tonight, however, the slow action suited her. Dinner with her sisters had left her surprisingly mellow. Maybe it was the beer.

"You gentleman need anything to drink?" she asked, passing by two men who were leaning against the smaller backup bar they only staffed on weekends. Both men shook their heads, one holding up a half-full bottle to indicate he had plenty, the other never taking his eyes off a couple of women on the dance floor.

Farther back in the corner, there was another duo of men, tossing darts at an electric board. As Vi got closer, she realized the bigger man looked familiar. "Brendan?"

The handsome man turned, giving her one of his wide smiles. "I know how you don't like being bothered at work, so I was staying out of your way."

"Thanks, but, as you can see, I can afford to stop and chat for a few minutes tonight."

"That's what I was hoping. This is my friend, Matt. He had a lousy week at work, so we thought we'd commiserate over a couple of beers."

She turned to say hi to the dark-haired man who was about the same age as her and Brendan. "Vi Mason, nice to meet you."

The stranger nodded. "I've heard a lot about you."

Unfortunately, she suspected he wasn't just being polite. Not that she minded Brendan talking about her, but she hoped he wasn't mooning over her. When they'd first met, they'd gone out for the occasional burger or movie, and it had escalated physically due to their mutual attraction. But she didn't have time for a relationship between classes and her weird work schedule. Even if she did, Brendan wasn't the kind of guy she saw herself with long-term. They'd just been having fun. Most of the time, guys were more than happy with the no-strings concept, but lately, she got the feeling Brendan was looking at her differently. As evidenced by little good luck cards before major exams and surprises, such as tonight's drop-in.

I need to call things off with him. If he wanted a more serious relationship, he should be free to find one with some nice girl who would appreciate his caring manner and stamina. But that was not a conversation to have in the middle of her shift.

"Can I get you anything else?" she asked.

Brendan beamed, holding up a nearly empty glass. "Absolutely. I'm only here as a paying customer tonight. Regular tips and everything."

Vi actually thought taking money from a guy she slept with was a little creepy, but he meant well. She flashed them a parting smile and went to get their drinks. Ears sharpened by trying to eavesdrop on her parents' closed-door conversations when she was younger picked up Brendan's comment as she moved away.

"Told you she was pretty, didn't I?"

Her heart sank. He was definitely infatuated.

"If you go for that type," his friend conceded begrudgingly.

What the hell "type" did he mean, Vi wondered as Crash fixed the two drinks. Not that it much mattered what some man she'd probably never see again thought of her.

She delivered the whiskey sours, managing not to wince when Brendan left her three times a normal tip. "Thanks. Nice," she added, watching his friend hit the bull's-eye.

He nodded, reaching for his glass.

Vi watched him for a moment, thinking that his features looked familiar. "Has Brendan introduced us before?"

Matt shook his head. "Dystopic Literature. We had the course together a couple of years ago."

Was that where she'd seen him? "Right. Sorry I couldn't place you."

"Why would you? I sat in the back, mostly regretting that no other literature credit had been open at the time I needed, and you sat front and center, usually interrupting the lecture to argue with the prof. We never really talked."

"Well, it was a big class," she recalled. "Nice to have met you now. I'll check on you boys later, okay?"

"Sure, we'll be here," Brendan said cheerfully. "I'm not going anywhere."

Vi sighed, thinking she shouldn't pick such a nice guy next time—she didn't want to hurt anyone. *So that leaves what, jerks?* Good plan. No wonder Neely and Savannah looked at her as if she was crazy whenever she offered unsolicited advice.

"I find it interesting," Vi said suspiciously, "that no one told me Mom, Aunt Jo and Aunt Carol were joining us until we were already here, with no way for me to get home."

Looking up over a nearby rack of bridesmaids' dresses, Leah laughed.

Neely ignored her friend. "Don't be silly, Vi. It wasn't a conspiracy—Savannah just thought I'd told you, and I thought she had. They wanted to see the wedding dress before I officially buy it."

"All right, but if Mom starts making whacked-out suggestions on what the bridesmaids should wear—"

"It's my wedding. How whacked out do you think I'm going to let her get?" Privately, though, Neely was more concerned over what her younger sister would deem appropriate for the ceremony than what Beth would select. She was glad she had Savannah and Leah to help run interference.

"I think they're here," Leah said, coming to stand behind Neely.

Sure enough, Savannah was headed their way, her mother and aunts in tow. Savannah had offered to stand up front and watch for them while Leah and Vi compared notes on bridesmaid selections.

"I know where the nearest bus stop is," Vi muttered.

Neely was uncertain if it was meant to be a threat, should their mother start driving Vi crazy, or if it was just a mantra Vi was using to help get her through the morning.

Taking a step forward, Neely smiled. "Hi, Mom. Glad you could—"

"Where's the ring?" Beth was already reaching for her daughter's hand. "I can't believe I'm practically the last one to see it."

Neely repressed a sigh. She and Robert had only purchased the engagement ring a few days ago. She'd never been a woman who wore much jewelry or cared about an exact number of carats, so she'd been surprised at the number of times this week she'd caught herself smiling at the square-cut diamond. The set they'd chosen was simple but elegant. His romanticism must be contagious because she was looking forward to sliding the matching gold band over his finger on their wedding day.

"It's lovely," her mother pronounced with a sigh. Both aunts agreed. Then, apparently, the moment had passed and Beth reverted to form. "I'm surprised you're not already putting on your dress, though. The sooner we get your final decision out of the way, the more time we have to find dresses for your attendants."

"Okay." Neely turned toward the room where a saleslady had already hung the reserved gown for her.

As Neely passed, Vi whispered, "Race you to the bus stop."

Neely didn't want to encourage her younger sister, but once alone in the dressing room, she laughed. Savannah came in to help her fasten the back, then Neely made her grand entrance. Well, as grand as one could be in the back of a store where your family was squashed together and your favorite aunt was digging through her purse to find coupons she'd clipped.

"Vi, do you ever bake?" Aunt Carol was asking. "You always had such a sweet tooth as a girl, and I have a coupon for a great cake mix. I'd give it to Savannah, but she never uses a mix."

"Thanks, Aunt Carol." Vi took the small rectangle of paper with a resigned sigh. "Oh, look, here's Neely."

Aunt Jo gasped, pressing her hands together beneath her chin. "Isn't she a vision?"

"Oh, Cornelia," Beth breathed.

Aunt Carol tilted her head. "Are you sure that's the one you want? There are a few specially discounted with damaged beading that you could get for half off. Between your mother and me, we could sew up any rips or snags."

Neely smiled. "No, this is the one I want. I was almost certain the other day, but now, after trying it on again…"

"Go up on the dais so you can see it in the three-way mirrors again," Savannah urged.

Neely did, enjoying the swish of satin and the way the dress made her feel. She glanced back to her loved ones, biting her lip when she noticed Leah wiping away a tear.

"Don't worry about me," her friend said. "This is happy crying. You look gorgeous."

"Yes, you do," Beth said, doling out rare praise. Then she turned to her oldest daughter. "Job well done, Savannah! I knew you'd help her pick out something perfect."

"Mama, Neely found the dress. Vi and I were just here to offer backup opinions."

But Neely didn't care who got the credit, only that everyone was in agreement that this was The Dress.

Maybe she had experienced flashes of resentment growing up, over Beth and Savannah's relationship, but as her sister had pointed out over their last dinner, she'd never *tried* to exclude Vi or Neely. Similarly, Neely had never tried that hard to find more common ground with their mother. It was just too bad Neely and Vi weren't closer in age—they could have kept each other company instead of Vi growing up alone in the house after her siblings were gone. And maybe if they'd been closer, Neely could have shared some of her own college experiences, helped Vi be less reckless at times, helped her find some direction.

"Well, now that's settled," Beth said, "we should find dresses for the bridesmaids. Jo pointed out something just lovely in yellow—"

"Mama," Savannah cut in before Vi could voice the objection that was clear on her face. "That's not always the most flattering shade for blondes. Now, Leah and I were thinking more along the lines of…"

Nearly an hour later and at the second shop of the day, Neely was thinking that it was kind of fun to have the shoe on the other foot. Instead of being the one trying on dress after dress and worrying about what would or wouldn't zip over her hips, she was the one standing outside and waiting for the fashion show.

"This one is too large," Vi called through the door.

"Could you ask the saleslady to bring me one the next size down?"

"Wait," Beth ordered, pushing aside the curtain. "Don't take that off yet, I want to check the fit. Oh for the love of…what *are* you wearing?"

Neely heard her sister sigh.

"It's a thong, mother. And I can tell whether or not a dress is too big for me."

"That's not proper underwear at all! What would people think if they knew you had that on under your clothes?"

"Well, most people don't just barge into the dressing room while I'm—"

"Vi, the saleswoman is back," Neely interrupted quickly. "What size was it you said you needed?"

It took another hour as some of the dresses they'd all liked on magazine pages were less flattering in reality, but eventually, they settled on a dress everyone liked. Almost everyone, anyway.

"It's *pink*." Vi glared from the raised dais where Beth had lined up the bridesmaids.

"The color's called ballet slipper," Neely corrected. "It's not truly pink. Would I do that to my redheaded best friend?"

"I think it's gorgeous," Savannah said, turning in front of the mirror and admiring the muted fabric that fell just below her knees. A satin ribbon of bright pink wrapped under her bustline, catching the light.

"It's very neutral and flattering to all of us," Leah agreed. "If it helps, Vi, think of it as taupe but much prettier."

"Because I'm such a fan of taupe," Vi muttered.

"You can all pick your own ribbon," Neely cajoled. "Savannah likes the bright pink accent, but Leah will probably go with something different. Navy or maybe celadon."

"What if I wanted purple, or polka dots?" Vi asked, a glint in her eye.

"It's your dress. I want a coherent bridal party, but you don't have to be clones."

"You'd honestly let me do polka dots?"

"Well, of course you aren't going to get polka dots," Beth said. "I can hardly tell anymore when that girl is joking. Is she joking?"

Vi sighed. "Yes, Mom, I was joking. I guess this isn't half-bad."

"Great, then we can start planning flowers and bouquets." Savannah clapped her hands together with apparent glee.

Leah grinned at Neely. "Your sister is having way too much fun with this."

"Weddings should be fun," Savannah argued. "Do

you guys know there's a bridal expo on the other side of town? I didn't say anything before because I wasn't sure we'd have time, but why keep looking if we've found a dress all of us can agree on?"

"Wait, I agree to wear pink to this wedding and we have to go do *more* bridal shopping?" Vi shot a beseeching glance at Neely. "Am I being punished for doing the right thing?"

"I know how you feel," Neely said. "I may be a dull accountant, but it still takes more than a swatch to excite me."

"It won't be so bad," Leah said. "Expos are fun. Free samples, the possibility of taking care of ninety percent of your wedding details under one roof, door prizes and since Robert isn't here showing us all how disgustingly happy he and Neely are, we can mock the sappy couples we pass."

"There's mocking?" Vi asked. "No one told me there was mocking. Count me in."

Beth sighed. "I wish we could join you, as well, but we have to get Jo back. She promised to help Darnell with the store. Leah, I meant what I said earlier about calling him if you're interested in a job. You just tell him I sent you."

"Thanks, Mrs. Mason, but I'm doing all right with the job I have."

"You deal with all of those female shoppers! You'd meet so many more men in a different career, and you're looking lovely these days."

"I appreciate that," Leah said, "but I'm not in any hurry for another romance."

"You're sure? Neely, has she met your brother? He's a nice single man."

"What about my Nick?" Carol asked. "He's unattached, as well."

Neely winced—they wanted to fix her best friend up with Douglas, the serial dating divorced man on the rebound or Nick, the compulsive gambler? She waited until her mom and aunts were saying goodbye to Savannah to assure Leah, "You're an intelligent, attractive woman. When you're ready, you'll find a guy who's worthy without anyone shoving him at you."

Leah pursed her lips. "I don't know. Maybe. I talk to women at the cosmetics counter and hear all kinds of dating horror stories. And a guy doesn't even have to be a creep to be all wrong for you. Lots of relationships fall apart even— Oh, Lord, I am the worst maid of honor ever."

"No, it's okay." Neely shook her head at her friend's stricken expression. "You're not telling me anything I haven't heard before. That's why Robert and I are discussing what kind of prenup we need. Well, not *need*, but you know what I mean."

"Yeah, I do. But I truly hope you never need it."

So do I. Neely glanced toward the twinkling engagement ring on her left hand, the diamond as bright as the future she and Robert would work to create.

By the time the women had strolled through the aisles in the first half of the convention center, Savannah sensed energy was flagging. The quartet-for-hire playing in a cubicle at the end of the row wasn't helping matters. As lovely as their violin concerto was, it was also slow, sleepy music. Neely was stifling yawns, and Leah had looked borderline weepy when they passed a keepsake vendor who showed them time capsule boxes meant to be enjoyed on a couple's first, fifth and tenth anniversary. Vi hadn't looked interested in anything since they'd passed the booth where neon spray-string had been suggested as an alternative to rice, confetti or bubbles.

Her eyes had lit up as she'd reached for one of the cans. "Oooh. Any chance we could spray this at the bride and groom as they head down the church steps?"

"None," Neely answered.

"I'm wearing pink for you," Vi reminded them all again. "You owe me."

"Hey, when it's your wedding, we'll cart in all the Silly String you want," Neely promised.

Now Neely looked as if she never wanted to hear the word *wedding* again. She had a plastic bag full of samples and accumulated business cards with notes scribbled on them, along with a few glossy color brochures for products or services she wanted to discuss with Robert.

"Flowers, pew bows and lace accessories are on the next aisle," Savannah said. "After that, we can rest for a bit. The center is a food court and a runway for periodic fashion shows. They also have drawings for honeymoon stays and romantic cruises."

"Don't sign up," Leah warned. "By the time you and Robert are married, you'll have been put on every catalog and commercial mailing list known to man. And a few known only to dogs. I still don't know how I got added to *Collars and Leashes Monthly* when I don't own a pet...but if it has anything to do with Phillip's extramarital activities, I would just as soon never find out."

Savannah halted, stunned by Leah's ability to reference her ex's infidelity so casually. Even *small* marital problems embarrassed Savannah; as if discussing them was admitting she'd failed.

Vi looked up from a lavender sheet of paper, the

printed map they'd been handed at the entrance. "If you change your mind, Leah, you might actually be able to pick up a nice collar on this last row. You did say you'd need a wedding present for the rat bastard?"

Leah laughed, and Savannah reached for the map, scouting skeptically for the row in question. Sure enough, it advertised vendors that sold "intimacy enhancements," as well as novelty items for bachelorette parties and adult fun for the newlyweds.

"My tired feet are suddenly rejuvenated," Vi said. "Let's get over there before all the good merchandise is taken."

Savannah didn't care what the map said—she doubted she'd find anything there that enhanced the intimacy in her marriage. Did any of the women with her suspect that part of her enthusiasm for the bridal expo stemmed from wanting an excuse not to go home? A lump formed in the back of her throat as she thought about the week she'd had.

For a day or so, she'd been so mortified over the conversation she'd overheard that she'd barely known what to say to Jason. So it became easier just to avoid him. By Thursday, it struck her that she hadn't really talked to him in days and *he hadn't even noticed.* Clearly if she ever wanted to punish her husband, the silent treatment would be ineffective.

But she wasn't looking to punish anyone. All she wanted was for things to be as they were, but she didn't know how to accomplish it. How could you fix something only one person thought was broken? He'd dismissed her request for them to do something alone together, and after he'd called her clingy and suggested to their son that they humor her, she wasn't inclined to initiate any romantic closeness. She suspected that even worse than not kissing your husband was wondering if his kissing you back was a favor brought on by warped chivalry.

"We lose you, Savannah?" Vi peered at her with concern.

"N-no. Just thinking about what kinds of bouquets we could put together," she lied. She caught the glances her sisters exchanged; although she knew they cared about her, the pity and worry still rankled, underscoring the mousy failure she feared she was becoming.

Leah, God love her, seemed oblivious. She not only accepted Savannah's fib, but used it to pay her a compliment. "You ever think about doing this professionally? You'd be a natural. I didn't have family nearby when I got married, and the church's wedding planner only orchestrated seating and the rehearsal. I could have used someone who knew what she was talking about to help me with the other details."

"As a business, wedding consulting has really taken off," Neely added. "Savannah, you're great at this frou-frou stuff."

"Thanks. I think."

Her sister tried again. "Seriously, Mom was right earlier. Without your advice, I'd probably still be looking for my gown, much less dresses for all of you to wear. And you think *I* know which men at the ceremony are supposed to get boutonnieres?"

Vi had caught their enthusiasm, was practically vibrating with it. "Think about it, aren't you going to have more time after Trent starts university in the fall? There are all kinds of business courses you could take to help get you started."

"Just because both of my children will be in college and *you're* apparently enrolled throughout perpetuity doesn't mean it's a feasible suggestion for me. Even with the boys gone, I'll be very busy with…with…" To Savannah's utter horror, tears welled up in her eyes. Watching Vi and Neely exchange another set of distressed looks through the blur only sharpened the sick feeling in her stomach. "I have to use the ladies' room."

No one stopped her as she hurried through the crowd, feeling her whole world splinter apart. This was like a nightmare. Some people dreamed about being back in high school unable to remember their locker combination, others tossed and turned plagued by images of being naked in public. Savannah had always feared making a fool of herself, doing the wrong thing. For her, losing it emotionally *was* being naked in public.

Her earliest memories involved Beth stroking her hair, murmuring, "You're my angel, my perfect little girl." She didn't remember when her parents had brought Neely home, but she did have flashes of toddlerhood or maybe the preschool years. Of Beth instructing Neely, "Watch Savannah, see how she does it?" Whether the "it" was coloring in the lines or using her spoon, she'd been the role model.

Maybe it was the same with all firstborns, and maybe some of them resented the pressure. Savannah had only felt special. Teachers in school had applauded her, as well. Other kids were artistic, yet temperamental, so good at math they could probably crack codes by the time they hit their teens yet lousy at English. Savannah's singular talent was that she'd been good at being good. Maybe no subject came easily to her and she wasn't destined for A-plusses, but she worked hard to earn A's in every class. She was a good student, a good daughter, as good a sister as she knew how to be. Then a good girlfriend, wife, housekeeper, mother, cook. The boys didn't need so much daily mothering now, though, and recently she felt as if she wouldn't be any help to Jason unless they were playing doubles golf or she became an obstetric nurse.

It was ludicrous to tell the girls she wouldn't have time for a job next fall when, truthfully, she was here today trying to kill as many hours as possible. She had other friends she could spend time with—fellow PTA moms and doctor's wives, but what if they asked about things between her and Jason? What if they relayed something sweet their husbands had done and it turned out that this strained, oddly disjointed phase of her marriage wasn't normal at all but just *her*?

Last week at lunch, Patsy Morrow, mother of three, had said she envied Savannah, sending her youngest to college. "Mike just started last year, and he's already decided he wants to move back home and finish at a local school to save money on housing. And I've still got four years before my youngest is off! You're so lucky, getting the house back so you and Jason can be alone."

Savannah had briefly wanted to stab darling Patsy with her soup spoon. So it was probably best to hold off on social lunches for a few more days.

She finally got up the nerve to check out her reflection in the ladies' room mirror and saw her face was red and blotchy. Great. She was fighting back tears so she wouldn't have to walk around with swollen eyes and smeared makeup, but she looked like hell anyway. Taking deep breaths, she pressed a moist paper towel to her skin.

A commode flushed behind her, and Savannah almost jumped when the door clanged open. A little old lady with blue-rinsed hair and a paisley blouse appeared. As she washed her hands, she shot Savannah a sympathetic glance.

"Have you tried Vitamin E, hon? It sure helped when I was going through the Change."

"I am not going through the Change," Savannah snarled. When had her hormones become a matter of widespread concern? First her husband and son, now total strangers.

She regretted her inhospitality immediately, but the woman was already shuffling out the door with surprisingly quick steps. Now she was alone. If she'd wanted that, she could have gone home.

"You okay?"

Not alone for long, she amended, craning her head to study Neely. "Humiliated. Let me ask you a question. If you have a cranky moment or perspire, does everyone around you assume it's menopause?"

Neely grinned. "Is that why the woman coming out warned me I probably shouldn't talk to the 'touchy gal' in here?"

"I didn't mean to snap at her. I know menopause is in my immediate future, but I would appreciate people not trying to make me any older than I already feel."

"You shouldn't feel old, Savannah. Have you looked in the mirror? You're gorgeous. You're also smart, competent, nurturing, all the things you've always had going for you. The biggest difference between you now and you twenty years ago is all the experience and wisdom you've acquired."

Savannah expelled all the tension in her body with a puffed-out breath. "Thank you. You're darling to say so, even if *wisdom* is a euphemism for 'old as dirt.' Wouldn't it be great if Vi and I could change places for a few weeks? She's fearless. If her life were in a rut, she'd make proactive changes, not quietly worry about it. And I could help give her the direction she seems to lack.

"Maybe that's what's wrong. For the first time in my life, I don't have a preset direction. Growing up, I wanted to make Mama and Daddy proud, especially whenever Douglas got into trouble. I felt like I was supposed to make up for it somehow. Throughout high school, I wanted to graduate, with honors, and get accepted to a decent college so I could meet a decent guy. Then I wanted Jason to propose. Then I wanted to become a mother. It's unsettling to realize you've *accomplished* your life goals. Sort of leaves you feeling like, okay, folks, that was the show. Thanks for coming, drive carefully and don't forget to take care of your servers."

Neely was quiet for a long moment, bracing her arms on the faux marble counter. Then she looked at her sister. "Lacking direction isn't why you want to trade places with Vi. You just want to be twenty-six again."

Savannah laughed. "That, too."

"Nothing's over. You've just reached a new beginning. Robert's mom said something about having to adjust to retirement and Robert being out of the house. All the sudden she had time alone with her husband. But they're making the most of it now, seeing the world. And she's got twenty-five years on you. My marrying Robert is a new beginning. Vi getting this latest degree—"

"Is just the beginning of her next degree?"

"Something like that. Why do you need a preset direction?" Neely reached inside her purse and pulled out one of the purple expo maps. Then she neatly tore it in half, quarters and eighths. "You can make up any path you want."

"Nicely put." Savannah arched a brow. "But when did you become free-spirited?"

"Me? I said *you* can make up any path you want. I'll stick to statistics, schedules and maps. In fact…you don't have any tape, do you?"

CHAPTER 11

Vi didn't remember Neely's friend being so cool the last time they'd crossed paths, but she and Leah were cracking up as they evaluated party favors for a bachelorette party.

"Can't you just imagine using these for the cocktails?" Bad pun on Leah's part, considering she was holding up a bag of plastic penis straws.

It was a tacky extravaganza—and the most fun Vi had had all day. The only thing dulling her enjoyment was that her sisters hadn't met up with them yet. After Savannah's startling retreat earlier, they'd all stood in silence for a minute before Neely declared she should be the one to talk to her.

"You sure you don't want me to do it?" Leah had asked, compassion in her soft voice. "If she's having trouble in her marriage…"

"I think she is, a little, but I think it's as much or more

the impending empty nest. No offense, but if the one divorced woman among us goes in to commiserate, we might be sending the subliminal message that we think her marriage is doomed. Why don't you two go find that row Vi was dying to investigate and we'll meet you there? Savannah might need the laughs. If she's in better spirits later, we can hit the flowers on our way out."

When Vi didn't comment on the straws, Leah said, "She'll be okay, you know."

"You must be psychic."

"Your sister had a minor meltdown, hasn't returned and you're frowning. Doesn't take Kreskin to put it together."

Vi skimmed her hand over blinking visors that pronounced titles like Bride, Groom, and Best Man in small multicolored lights. "So if you don't have any extraordinary mental powers, how can you be so sure Savannah will be okay?"

"Well, for one thing, I think Neely's right and part of this is empty nest—Savannah will be fine after the initial adjustment. Must be tough to have labored so long to be a good mother only to have all your children gone. But as difficult as the short term might be, I'm sure there are long-term benefits. Even if it is something worse, she has you and Neely to help her through it. How could she not be okay?"

A month ago, Vi would have laughed derisively at the suggestion that she could be of assistance to her perfect older sister. But she'd been changing her mind about a lot of things lately.

A few minutes later, Vi watched her sisters approach and decided Leah must be right. "Looks as if they're both smiling. That's a good sign, right?"

"Or they got free samples from the guy who rents out the champagne fountain and margarita machines."

Vi knew instinctively that Savannah, who always managed to say the right thing, would never ask a woman last seen bolting in tears if everything was all right. She'd try to find a cheerful, tactful way to draw the person back into conversation as if nothing had ever happened. It was the type of technique Vi would have eschewed in the past, since pretending something hadn't occurred seemed sillier than tackling it head-on. But this was for Savannah's sake—besides, Vi was always up for trying something new.

So she flashed a wide smile. "Savannah, you have got to see all the stuff we've found for Neely's bachelorette party. I'm definitely getting my revenge for the pink."

Savannah obligingly leaned over to peer at all of the atrocious games and badges people apparently subjected their closest friends to when celebrating that friend's decision to marry. Maybe it was proof of love.

You could tell the guy later, if you were fighting over whose turn it was to do the dishes, for instance, "I think you should do this one little thing for me. Do you know how badly I let my friends embarrass me just so I could go through the traditional rites of becoming your wife?"

Neely's eyes widened at the sight of a mock bridal veil. The "jewels" adorning the tiara were a rainbow of condoms showing through clear cellophane. "You guys cannot let Vi plan this."

"Oh, please. You should have seen the straws *Leah* wanted to get. I'm the lesser of your two evils here."

Neely groaned. "That's the most frightening thing I've ever heard in my life."

"Only because you've never received a college tuition bill," Savannah said. "Those are terrifying."

Vi nodded, pointing toward her head. "I went platinum because writing the check last semester turned it all white, anyway."

"If Vi is planning the bachelorette party, I think it's up to us to tackle a bridal shower," Savannah told Leah.

"Does anyone else think it's weird," Neely asked aloud, "that my announcing one social event, the wedding, has spawned about fourteen other social events? We've got the barbecue coming up, apparently a bridal shower, a bachelorette party…. No wonder people go on honeymoons. They're exhausted by then and need the vacation to sleep."

Vi rolled her eyes. "If that's really what you think honeymoons are for, Robert has my sympathy." She pointed toward an open suitcase labeled Naughty Trousseau to illustrate her meaning.

Still standing close, Savannah elbowed her aside to take a look. "This is only meant to be a gag gift, right? No one would actually wear any of these."

"Definitely not me," Neely said with a shudder before Leah invited her to check out an automated doll in a tuxedo called the Wedding Heckler. He had all sorts of humorous comebacks for the "speak now" portion of the ceremony.

Vi studied the clothes with Savannah. "I don't know. The vinyl skirt might work with the right shoes and top."

"If you're a *hooker*," her sister retorted. "And there's something seriously wrong with the underwear."

"Crotchless. That's on purpose. So are the cutouts in the bra."

Savannah shook her head, backing away. "I know you're just supposed to wear them in front of the guy who's about to see you naked anyway, but…"

"No, I agree. Those are so not you—no one wants to see you in vinyl less than me. But you could take the occasional risk. Nothing that would get you arrested, just a shorter skirt for a change. Serve Jason a romantic dinner at home in lingerie. If I can wear pink, you could wear something trashy just once."

"Trashy? I don't even have to argue that. The word pretty much sums up my objections already."

Vi shouldn't have used the slang one of her girlfriends substituted for hot. "I misspoke. All I really meant was—"

"Cheap?"

"You're the one who talks about catching flies. Think of seductive clothes as visual honey."

Savannah's lips turned up in a half grin. "Not bad, as far as arguments go. But you're talking about catching men, and I'm married. I don't think those would have the desired effect on Jason, anyway. How much good can showing up half-naked do when the man sees naked women for a living? More importantly, there's a difference between looking sexy for your husband and looking like a desperate and neglected housewife in a pathetic ploy for attention."

The words *neglected* and *pathetic* stood out, making Vi's heart hurt for her sister. "Forget Jason. Other men, too. I know you and Mom have complained that I don't worry enough about what people think, but I like wearing clothes *I'm* comfortable in, ordering what I really want off the menu, even if I run the risk of my date thinking I'm a pig. Don't change a thing about your wardrobe—or your life—if you truly like it. But don't stay in a rut just because you're afraid to try something different, Savannah."

For a few minutes, her sister said nothing, merely stared into space as if she were trying to imagine things she could change, ways her life could improve. Then she turned to Vi with a sudden grin. "Were you always this smart, or is that college of yours just really good?"

"What did you say to her?" Neely asked. Savannah, standing in the aisle with Leah and plotting the bridal shower, was actually smiling. Neely had tried to cheer her up in the ladies' room, but hadn't been nearly as successful as Vi. Ever since the two sisters had walked away from the last booth, Savannah had seemed less troubled.

Vi raised her gaze from the sign-up sheet she'd been considering. "I just told her to take some chances, try something new."

"That's what I said, too, more or less. I even had a visual aid—tore up a map and everything."

"You mean we gave her the same advice?" Vi laughed. "Does this mean we're starting to think alike?"

"No. Case in point, don't bother trying to talk me into this class."

"It's a seminar. And I thought it would make a nice gift for you and Robert." She held up an informational brochure on tantric sex. "Think of it as yoga for your love life."

Neely took the brochure, mostly to get it away from her sister and end the discussion. "What *is* your fascination with other people's love lives lately?"

"It's not a fascination. I'm just… I'm not an idiot, I know marriage is hard. Seems to me this is one way to try to stay closer so you can fight all of the stuff that comes at you as a unit instead of fragmented individuals. When I hear about people getting divorced, they rarely say, 'And we were having hot, intensely connected sex, so I was shocked when he ran off with his secretary.' They usually describe having drifted apart first."

"This really worries you, huh?"

"Well, not for myself. I've never been in a relationship long enough to drift. But Douglas and Zoe? I hated that they split up."

Neely doubted lack of passion had been Douglas and Zoe's problem, but it was true he could have saved himself some heartache by being better attuned to his wife.

Vi continued, her voice agitated. "Now even *Savannah* is having problems! You grew up in a different generation, a more innocent time, but half my classmates came from divorced households."

More innocent time? Neely flashed to Watergate, Vietnam and Ted Bundy, but didn't argue the point. The focus here was the revelation that marriage scared Vi.

A thought struck her. "Mom and Dad didn't fight, did they? I mean, after all the rest of us left home?"

Vi glanced at her interlocked hands, wiggling her fingers. "Not in front of me. They barely interacted except for Mom telling him it was time for dinner or that he should talk to me about my punching a boy at school or he should take the trash out—you know how she is. Sometimes I heard hushed voices at night when it sounded like they were having tense conversations."

"Tense or just serious?" Neely asked. They would have had lots of things to discuss, not the least of which was Vi and her scrapes with authority.

When Vi was about nine, Beth had lost her father to a stroke and shortly after, the Masons had made the decision to put Beth's mother in a retirement home. Then there were finances. Beth could march up to a stranger on the street and offer an unsolicited opinion on the way that person was living her life, but her Southern pride precluded worrying about money in front of others, especially the children who depended on her. Neely could think of dozens of things her parents might have discussed behind closed doors.

Had they ever guessed that Vi, with no siblings left at home to reassure her, worried about their marriage? "They weren't necessarily arguing, you know."

"I guess not. They just never seemed close. Have you ever seen him kiss her? And I didn't mean Mom and Dad specifically had problems. I just think affection is like an extra layer of insurance around a marriage."

She thought about her argument that a prenup was insurance and wondered if her sister's approach kept a marriage healthier. "That's not bad advice, and I'll keep it in mind. But honestly, Robert and I are pretty happy in that department without Ben's balls and other weird props."

For a moment, Vi's face was blank. "Ben-Wa."

"Wa...tever. The point is, you don't have to worry about us, okay?"

Vi grinned. "Okay."

Neely sighed with relief. Maybe now they could move on to flower arrangements—boy, there was something she never thought she'd actually look forward to. Everyone was smiling simultaneously, all threatening emotional crises averted.

Leah had assured her it was normal for the *bride* to

get more neurotic as the big day approached. Unfortunately for her poor sisters, it appeared to be catching.

Neely punched in her security code, waited for the gate arm to lift and steered her car into the complex. It had been a long, but productive, day.

"I can't wait to get out of these shoes," she told Leah. "And maybe take a bubble bath." Would Robert want to join her, if he was still there?

"Yeah, I'm ready to go home and tuck myself into bed, so I won't stick around. Call me when the invitations arrive and I'll help you with the calligraphy. Whatever you do, proofread them carefully before we start stuffing envelopes. You never know what errors might get made at the printer's, and you don't want to announce the wedding of Robert and Cornelius or something."

Neely laughed. "Definitely not, thanks for the tip. And all your help today."

"My pleasure. It was nice to get out with other people. Do you think I should do that more? Go out."

"Do you mean with people, or men?"

"I guess if I can't even say it, I'm not ready. Sometimes, I think about how badly he hurt me and doubt I'll ever be able to trust another man enough to have a healthy relationship. Other times I think, I don't want to be alone for the rest of my life."

"No reason it has to be decided now, though, right? Leave yourself open to possibilities, but don't rush into anything." It was the best advice Neely had to give.

Leah smiled. "Sounds good, but promise me you won't let your mother try to set me up with anyone."

"I swear." Spotting a red truck with mud-covered wheels and a gun rack drew Neely up short. It was sitting in her parking spot. Each apartment had two assigned spaces, and hers were currently filled by Robert's car and...*Stuart.*

Stuart was one of Robert's oldest friends, a big-hearted good ole boy whose neck was as red as his truck. To be honest, she'd never been entirely comfortable around the bearlike man. He was nice enough, but his jokes tended to be obnoxious if not outright offensive and she always had the impression he might smack her on the bottom if she turned her back to him. He was the kind of man who genuinely didn't understand why a woman might not want to be called sugar or sweet thang. His idea of a heartfelt compliment included telling other men's spouses, "You look hot enough to fry up sausages."

But loving Robert meant accepting his friends, too. She'd come to terms with that over the past six months. It was just that, usually, his friends were at *his* place and if she wanted to escape, she could go home. Thinking again about the house-hunting excursion planned for tomorrow, she supposed those days were over.

"Guess I'll see you back to visitor parking," Neely said, tapping the accelerator. "Stuart's here."

"Friend of Robert's?"

"Yeah. Met in college. Stuart dropped out, but the friendship remained."

"Robert's a loyal guy. I know I mouth off about marriage sometimes, but you got one of the good ones."

Neely found a space that put her car bumper to bumper with Leah's.

"So, just for future reference, is this Stuart cute?" Leah asked as she opened her door.

"Not exactly." Neely thought about his grizzled beard, understated beer belly and tendency to share rambling anecdotes that all ended with the unintentionally ironic, "Long story short..." "He's lovable in his own way, but not someone I would categorize as attractive. But the fact that you even asked is probably a good sign that maybe you'll be able to date again one day."

"Maybe. One day."

The two women said their goodbyes, and Neely carried a bag of samples and informational brochures in one hand and a bigger bag filled with silk flowers and bits of lace in the other. Neither was heavy, though, and she juggled them pretty easily to open her front door.

Both men stood as she came in.

"Hey," Robert said, beaming at her.

It was nice to return home to someone who looked so happy to see you.

"The future ball-and-chain," Stuart said by way of greeting. "You need any help with those bags? I'd be happy to go out to your car if there are more to bring in."

"Thanks, but this is all of it." Just a few ideas to run by Robert so she could call Savannah this week with final decisions. She set everything on the kitchen table.

"Sorry I'm in your spot," Stuart said. "Didn't mean to stay this long, but we got caught up in a John Wayne marathon. I'm fixin' to go."

"You don't have to leave on my account," she said. "I'm headed back to take a shower, so if the two of you weren't finished with the movie…"

"Nah, *The Cowboys* is on now, and it's not one of my favorites," Stuart told her. "Hard to love a movie where the Duke doesn't at least make it to the end. But I'll see you at your parents' barbecue, if not sooner."

Her parents' barbecue? Oh. That probably should have occurred to her—she needed to get more in the habit of thinking of Robert's friends and family as well as hers. After all, Leah was one of the first people she'd invited. *Friends and family?* Should she invite Zoe to the wedding? The engagement party? They'd all liked her sister-in-law, but she didn't want Douglas to be uncomfortable. She'd have to ask Savannah about the protocol.

Robert dropped his arm around her shoulders. "Why don't I take your keys and move the car while you shower?"

"That would be appreciated." She fished her key chain from her purse. "Bye, Stuart."

"Bye. And y'all don't forget to call me if you need help moving. No sense paying one of them companies if you can round up enough guys with trucks."

She thanked him for the offer, then breathed in the quiet once both men had gone out the front door. The day had left her with sensory overload. A hot shower would clear her head.

When she emerged from the bathroom in her favorite terry-cloth robe, she found Robert sitting on the side of her bed, two glasses of white wine on her nightstand.

He patted the comforter. "I thought I could give you a foot massage while you told me how the wedding plans are coming. Least I could do since you were out there putting it all together while Stuart and I were kicking back here."

A happy sigh escaped her. "Watch it, I could get used to this."

He grinned. "That's the idea. If we're going to start looking at homes tomorrow, I want you to be sure I'm the guy you want to be sharing a house with."

The mattress sagged under her weight as she joined him. "I don't have any doubts, you know."

He kissed her, tasting like the chardonnay he'd poured for them. "So how *are* the wedding plans going?" he asked, swiveling her legs around so that her foot was between his warm hands.

"Pretty well." She realized she sounded surprised by this and smiled. "For two previously obnoxious sisters and one divorced friend, they really know how to put together a ceremony. Savannah is invaluable. She sent me home with some buds and ribbon to show you, and if you don't absolutely hate the colors, she's going to put together a small bouquet for me. We've decided to use silk for me and let each of the girls just carry one long-stemmed fresh flower apiece. They can place them in vases when they reach the altar. Simple, but elegant. And as Aunt Carol would gleefully point out, not too expensive. Vi's been really helpful, too, even agreeing to wear a bridesmaid's dress she considers pink, but…"

"But what?"

"I don't know." Neely tried to form the nebulous impressions she'd gathered today into a coherent thought.

She'd never realized marriage made her sister nervous. "She has some weird ideas. She insists you and I will stay together longer if I'd try out some kinky sexual scenarios. Seemed really shaken up by the thought of divorce, and I didn't think much shook her."

Robert shrugged. "Her big brother's marriage failed, and you told me that Savannah has hit a rough patch. Vi's the youngest in the family. Can you imagine how hard it would be for her if our marriage didn't do well? If none of her three siblings could make it work, what could she possibly think *her* chances are?"

"But it's independent probability, really. Whether any of us succeed or fail has no direct bearing on whether the rest of us do." More importantly, Vi by her own admission had slept with plenty of men, yet had few serious relationships. Good sex was nice, but sooner or later, her sister was going to have to make an emotional investment if she wanted something lasting.

"Independent probability?" Robert grinned. "Mathspeak is such a turn-on."

She raised her eyebrows. "Then clearly something is wrong with you."

"Or I'm very much in love. By the way." He pressed a kiss to the arch of her foot, kneading her calf muscle with skilled fingers and rubbing his thumb over her sensitive skin. "I'd be willing to make the sacrifice of trying one or two of those kinky suggestions. For the greater good, of course."

She would have made a snappy comeback if little currents of electric bliss weren't traveling through her body, starting where he touched her. She knew from experience when and how they would end, and the thought made inner muscles clench with pleasure. Her exhaustion forgotten, she slid her foot off his lap, her legs on either side of him, and tugged him down to the bed with her.

For the greater good, of course.

CHAPTER 12

"What do you think?" Leslie Kent asked, her hand once again fluttering to Robert's arm. The brunette had an annoying habit of deferring to his opinion as if Neely wouldn't also be living in whatever house the couple purchased.

To his credit, Robert disentangled himself gracefully, sidestepping the chirpy real estate agent. "Neely and I are going on the deck for a moment, to check out the view and discuss everything."

"Sure. You two take your time." The woman was already reaching for her cell phone to check messages.

Neely followed him onto the wooden balcony, happy to have the door closed between them and Leslie.

"What do *you* think?" Robert asked.

"Like the house. Can't stand her."

He grinned. "She can be a bit much."

"I haven't touched you as much today as she has."

The agent had been a bit sycophantic during their initial consultation, but perhaps since she'd been on one side of the desk and Robert and Neely the other, Neely hadn't realized that she was only really sucking up to half of them.

"Maybe she thinks that as the man, I have the deciding financial vote that will determine what she takes home in commission."

Or maybe she was just drawn to him. She wouldn't be the first woman who'd noticed that he was distinguished, successful and attractive. His neighbor, Sheila, for instance was borderline flirtatious, but Neely had never been the jealous type. How could she be when Robert was so demonstrative about his own feelings toward her?

"Enough about her," she said. "How do we feel about the houses?"

Whatever else she could say about Leslie, the woman had done a great job locating available properties that met all of their criteria. Neely had worried they wouldn't see anything today that they both loved and could afford. Instead, of the six homes they'd seen so far, she loved two of them and liked a third, all in their budget range. There was something to be said for having saved up a nice-size nest egg before buying a home.

"This one's not bad," he said. "Impressive closet

space, but I'm not wild about the yard. Going from no lawn care to being responsible for a hillside of grass will be an adjustment. And the steep slope might hurt its resale value. I can't imagine anyone with small children would want to buy a house where the slightest misstep could send their kid plummeting into the street."

She nodded. "I liked the last one better. And I know prevailing wisdom would caution against making an offer on the first house you see, but…I loved that one."

It had been their favorite, the standard against which they measured all those that followed.

"Yeah. She hit the nail on the head with that one. What if we go back for a second look? A really hard look to see if we missed something."

Leslie drove them back to the charming brick one-story, with its graceful columns on either side of the front door and its Motivated Seller sign in the modest-size, perfectly level, yard. They searched for flaws they might have overlooked, but Neely came away from the second showing with an even more favorable impression. She could easily picture them here together, with her bed in the master bedroom and his entertainment center in the corner of the sunny living room.

After sleeping on it, they called Leslie in the morning with instructions to make an offer. Halfway through lunch, the phone rang.

Neely rose from the table. "Hello?"

"Leslie Kent here. Is this Neely?"

Unexpectedly nervous—had another offer come in before theirs, or were they about to be one step closer to their new life together?—Neely nodded, then realized the agent couldn't see her. "Yes, it is." She gestured Robert closer to the phone.

"The vendors were very pleased with your offer and are willing to throw in a couple of extras I routinely request," Leslie said. "If you'd like, we can go ahead and schedule an inspection. We can also keep looking while we wait, just in case you would like to have a Plan B. Not to be a negative Nancy, but sometimes things fall apart last minute. And there is one teensy catch, of sorts. The Willards are so motivated because they're being transferred out of the country and would like to have everything done quickly. Can we all agree on a closing date in early April, assuming the attorneys fit it in?"

"I'll talk to Robert, and we'll call you back. Thanks, Leslie." There would be penalties when they broke their leases, but the sooner they were paying one combined house payment a month, the more they would save.

Her pulse fluttered as she thought about everything they would need to do. *One thing at a time.* Surely that motto could get her through whatever hiccups arose—come hell, a wedding, moving, siblings or high water.

When the phone rang Wednesday evening, Vi considered letting the machine get it. Since she'd been legitimately busy, she hadn't returned Brendan's last message. But that was cowardice. Best to let him know that their casual romantic association had stopped being romantic and nudge him toward freedom.

She picked up the receiver. "Hello?"

"Hi. It's me, Savannah."

A month ago, if her sister had called out of the blue, Vi's first reaction would have been to ask, "Who's in the hospital?" Now, however, she merely settled into the plush cushions of the love seat, getting comfy. "Hi. How's your week going?"

"Pretty well, actually. I've, um, thought a lot about your advice. And I've already been out twice this week, once to play tennis with Dr. Schulmann's wife, then to take a friend a homemade cake for her birthday. She said it was so good I should charge people for them."

Vi frowned. "Sounds nice, but...wasn't that already a typical week for you?"

"Yes and no. Here recently, I've avoided doing things with some of the other wives in my circle. It's nice to be out of self-imposed solitary confinement. And I didn't tell you the best part yet. As part of my friend's birthday celebration, I took her on a mini shopping spree." Savannah lowered her voice to a conspiratorial whisper. "I bought some new clothes."

Only her sister would make a few wardrobe additions sound like a sinful secret.

Knowing that big changes often stemmed from small ones, Vi stifled her chuckle. "Nothing too radical?"

"No, just colorful. There's no law saying I have to wear pastel all the time or that every formal function requires a *black* evening dress, right?"

"That's the spirit!"

"It's not the only reason I called. Leah and I are going to start exchanging e-mails about a bridal shower, which we'll probably have at my place. Do you want to be included? I don't want you to feel obligated since you have such a busy schedule, but I didn't want you to feel left out, either."

"Thank you, but you two go ahead. You'll plan a much better shower than I could, and Neely deserves the best."

"Speaking of Neely, did you hear they've put an offer on a house?"

"I did, actually. I was at work when she called, but she left a message on my machine." It was unexpectedly nice to be kept in the family loop, which suddenly made her wonder, "Did she think to call Douglas, too? I know the three of us have been spending a lot of time together, but—"

"She had lunch with him yesterday. Filled him in on the house, asked him to be a groomsman and apparently got his opinion on Zoe being invited to the wedding and relevant celebratory occasions."

Vi bit her lip. "What did he say about that?"

"That Zoe was once part of this family and it would take more than a legal document to erase that. Neely teased him about it being an ironic thing for a lawyer to say. I'm sure if Zoe and Douglas cross paths, the two of them can be civil."

Civil? Was Vi the only one who knew that about six months after the divorce, Zoe and Douglas had bumped into each other at a mutual acquaintance's party and gone home together? Douglas had been high as a kite for two weeks afterward, thinking they might work things out. When the same personality conflicts that ended their marriage prevented them from getting back together, Douglas had been heartbroken. Vi had spent all her free evenings for a month—not that there had been many—eating takeout with him and trying to cheer him up. He'd insisted he'd learned his lesson, but one time when she'd called about a ride to their parents', she could have sworn she'd heard

Zoe's voice in the background. She'd never asked him about it or mentioned it to anyone else.

Vi chose her words carefully. "I wasn't worried about them arguing at the wedding, I was more worried about the emotional impact of the event. Sometimes, I'm not sure he's over her."

"Oh. I don't know, Vi. He's been dating quite a bit since the holidays."

Quite a bit, Vi thought to herself after she got off the phone with her sister. From what she knew, Douglas's social calendar verged on the frenetic. Was he looking for a replacement for his affections, or just trying not to think about Zoe?

She hadn't even put the cordless phone back in its cradle when it rang again, making her jump. *Okay, it will be just too weird if that's Douglas or Neely.*

It wasn't. "Vi? Hey, it's Brendan."

"Hey." She sighed. "Sorry I haven't called you back, but there is something I wanted to talk to you about."

Maybe she should worry less about her brother's romantic choices and invest more energy in trying to make better ones herself.

"Hey, looking good, Mom."

Savannah paused in fastening her earring, flashing a smile at her son. He stood restlessly in the doorway of her room, probably about to ask if he could borrow the SUV. No doubt he'd rather use his dad's car, but they were taking that to the children's charity benefit tonight—just as soon as Jason got out of the shower and was dressed. Besides, she felt her son was better protected by all of the SUV's safety features and figured teenage boys were less likely to hot-rod through traffic while driving something roughly the size of a city block.

The only thing that gave her pause about the Tank was all the backseat space. How must his girlfriend's parents feel when Trent picked her up, their only child tripping down the sidewalk toward a vehicle you could probably fit a water bed in? Still, there was little point in not trusting the kids. With Savannah and Jason gone tonight, the house would be empty if the two teenagers were determined to find a bed.

She sighed. "Was the compliment to butter me up before asking for the keys?"

"No, I think you look nice," he said indignantly. Then he smiled, showing the charm he'd inherited from his father. "And if I *was* buttering you up, it would be to ask if Steve could crash here tonight. I know it's last minute, but his sister is having a slumber party. He called begging refuge from all the squealing little girls. He said he could bring his PlayStation and a couple of his best discs so we could do a marathon. I know you're convinced too much of that will rot my brain and give me premature carpal tunnel syndrome, but any chance we can play games and eat junk food until dawn?"

Laughing, she crossed the room to engulf her son in a hug. Just when she was worried he wanted car keys and independence, possibly to go out and seduce young women, he surprised her by asking if a buddy could come over and play digital shoot-'em-up games.

"Absolutely," she said. "I'll even give you a twenty for pizza." Tiny price to play for a glimpse of her little boy inside the man he was fast becoming.

"Uh…thanks, Mom." He was obviously startled by the enduring hug, but one did not comment on a parent's weird behavior when that parent was offering to spring for food.

She straightened. "Go call Steve back. I have to holler at your father that we're running late. Oh, and *just* you and Steve while we're not here, okay? I don't want to come back to find one of those crazed parties they're always showing in teen movies."

"Got it." Trent laughed. "No crazed parties, check."

Turning toward the master bathroom, she caught her reflection in the vanity mirror. A well-dressed woman grinned back at her, looking younger than her age. More importantly, *feeling* younger than her forty-five years. The violet dress she wore tonight was a modest length, but it was the first strapless dress she'd worn out in a long time. She liked the vivid color and the smattering of sequins that randomly dotted the bodice. Her hair was pulled back, showing off the diamond earrings Jason had given her for their tenth anniversary.

He was a good husband, she thought, recalling jewelry she'd received through the years, his saying that he wanted to spoil her and make her feel as lucky as he was. He constantly praised her mothering skills with the boys, affirming the most important job she'd ever had. Maybe he hadn't been the most sensitive husband in the world lately, but shouldn't fresh starts apply to both of them? If she was finding new directions in her life, she didn't need petty grudges holding her back.

"Jason?" She pounded on the door to be heard over the running water. The faucet was turned off, and she heard the metallic slide and *whoosh* of the shower curtain being opened.

"Just need five minutes," he called through the door. "I'll drive fast to make up for it."

And she'd been worried about her *son* zipping across freeways? "Tell me which tie you want, and I'll pull it out of the closet."

"The burgundy. That will look okay with the suit, right?"

"It's a black suit. You don't own a tie that wouldn't look okay."

Was it progress that this was the longest conversation they'd had all week?

Her husband exited the bathroom, preceded by a waft of steam and the scent of his cologne. Damp, his hair was almost as dark as the slacks he wore. He was in the process of buttoning his shirt when he looked up and scowled.

"What's wrong?" she asked, glancing at her hand to make sure she held the right tie.

"Nothing. Is that what you're wearing?"

The man had graduated from medical school. Surely he wasn't so obtuse that he thought she was just whimsically trying on outfits to see what fit when they were already running late. "Of course it's what I'm wearing. I got dressed while you were shaving and am just waiting on you."

He said nothing. Nor did he make any motions to finish getting dressed.

"Jason, is there a problem with what I'm wearing?" Unless her zipper had suddenly come down, she couldn't imagine why he was still scowling. But the zipper was in the back, out of his line of sight, and she suspected she would have noticed a sudden draft against her spine. "Jason?"

Maybe he'd slipped on the soap and hit his head on the shower tile.

"Hmm? Oh, sorry. You look fine. Just a little different. I should probably get finished so we can leave."

"Yes." She held out the tie, feeling childish as she added, "*Trent* thought I looked very nice. Went out of his way to say so."

Jason nodded absently. "You raised polite boys, we have good reason to be proud."

He departed back into the bathroom and she glanced again at the dress. Maybe she'd been fooling herself that she looked good, younger. Was the color too bright, the neckline too low? *Perhaps I should change.* She had time if she hurried.

But as she reached for the closet door, she remembered the admiration in Trent's tone, the urging in Vi's that Savannah find new ways to make herself happy, regardless of what anyone else thought.

Perhaps it was just time Jason realized some things *were* going to be a little different.

CHAPTER 13

According to the traditional adage, March was supposed to go "out like a lamb." Meek, cheerful, cuddly. As she dug through her desk looking for aspirin, Neely thought whoever had come up with that stupid saying should be prosecuted for false advertising. Her March had stormed out in a huff, ringing in an even crankier April.

For a brief shining moment, she and Robert had been closer than ever, all the wedding plans were on track and she'd thought moving would go smoothly. Turned out, falling in love with the first house she'd seen had only been the deceptive setup for a false sense of security. The inspection had unearthed a few glitches, such as a plumbing problem that would only get worse with time and some irregular wiring where the current home owner had tried his untrained hand at electrical work, complicating matters for anyone who came after him. Robert and Neely had gone on two other outings with Leslie—both of which had included Leslie simpering at him—but hadn't found another house they liked as much. Negotiations for what the current owner was willing to do to compensate for the areas that would need repair were rapidly becoming a pain in the ass with the scheduled closing date on the line.

Meanwhile, she and Robert were…under stress. Assuming this closing went through smoothly, they should move in the near future. She'd suggested they start discussing what they wanted to keep in the new place and what they wanted to get rid of, and the man was being unreasonable! He seemed physically incapable of letting go of anything.

She wasn't unfeeling—she knew their home should be a combination of her furnishings, his and some brand-new belongings they picked out together. For instance, it made sense that they give up her television set. Both of his were more technologically advanced, so she voted they keep them, even though she'd never be able to figure out his convoluted remote controls. But Robert, it seemed, was unwilling to part with anything, including the hula lamp his parents had bought him when he was in college and had been going through some sort of tacky bachelor pad phase.

Since then, they'd apparently sought out unique or even outright tacky household items to give him. It was either a Walsh inside joke or they actually thought he used those cow-patterned coffee mugs that had udders on the bottom. He acted as if his parents might show up for a spot check and ask to see the dogs-playing-poker coasters or turtle clock, which seemed unlikely since they almost never came to his apartment and were rarely even in-state.

Every time Neely suggested something that he could gift to Stuart or throw out because it was well past its prime, Robert responded with lists of reasons he couldn't possibly part with it. It was reaching the point where negotiations over the house sale were actually easier than negotiations over what would go *in* the house.

To make matters worse, yesterday evening they'd had their first appointment with the marital attorney Douglas had suggested. The man gently pointed out that it wasn't ethical to represent both of them, and she belatedly realized Douglas had been recommending a lawyer for *her* to use. Robert needed his own. The entire situation and resurrected subject of prenuptial agreements had put Robert in a grim mood. He'd hardly spoken on the drive to her apartment.

Once they arrived, he'd asked, "Do you want me to come in?"

Feeling put on the spot and irritated that he wouldn't make the decision himself, she'd snapped, "Maybe that's not such a good idea tonight."

He'd left with a wounded look in his eyes, and she'd tossed and turned last night feeling alternately resentful and guilty. This morning, she'd acknowledged that both of them simply had a lot on their plates right now and had gone to his office to make peace with fresh coffee and some blueberry muffins, only to find him on the phone chuckling at something their real estate agent had said and where the *hell* was her aspirin when she needed it?

Neely banged the drawer shut and leaned back in her chair, breathing hard. Perhaps what was really needed here was to take a moment and regain perspective. Count to ten or chant a mantra or check her e-mail for forwarded jokes. Life was fine, she was fine.

Since most of the stuff people forwarded her seemed to get caught in her spam filters and she didn't actually have a mantra, she reached for her phone instead, dialing Leah's cell number from memory. She didn't know what her friend's schedule was today, but if she was at work, she'd have the phone off anyway, so Neely wouldn't be interrupting.

Thankfully, Leah answered. "Hello?"

"Hey. It's me." When she realized how often she'd

called her best friend to gripe in the last seventy-two hours, she sheepishly added, "Again."

Leah's laugh was knowing. "Don't sweat it. Weddings are stressful. So is moving. If you had a flawless house closing, you could never tell anyone about it because they'd all hate you."

"Oh, good, then all my friendships should be safe after this. Do me a favor?"

"Anything. I'd even wear pink for you," she added in a fair imitation of Vi.

"Remind me that I love Robert, that he's a wonderful guy and that I want to spend the rest of my life with him."

"Wow, must have had some fight if you're looking to your bitter divorced friend for affirmation."

"You're not bitter, at least, not without good reason. And it wasn't a fight, exactly. Just…mounting tension."

She supposed she could play the make-up sex card again, except that it would be a lot like Savannah's opinion of drinking. Instead of a hangover there would be afterglow, which was admittedly nicer, but wouldn't the same underlying problems still be there when they were done?

"The stress is normal," Leah promised. "You just need a chance to relax. Can you take an afternoon off work?"

"Are you kidding? I've already got time off scheduled for meeting the attorneys about the house and getting our marriage license. And I'm so behind, it's ridiculous! Not to mention my own personal taxes are due in about ten days." She could file for an extension, but would rather get them out of the way so she could focus on the other chaos. "I don't think taking the afternoon to navel-gaze and let more work accumulate will lower my stress level. But I could squeeze in a long lunch. Care to join me? My treat."

"Um…I would, but I already have plans to meet Savannah."

"My sister?"

"Yeah."

She waited a beat to see if she'd be invited to join them. "Oh." There was a good chance they were planning to talk about her or the bridal shower, so maybe it would be best if she didn't go, anyway.

"You know who you should take to lunch? Robert. Kidnap him from his office, take him somewhere nice and make goo-goo eyes at each other over a leisurely meal. It could do wonders for both your moods."

"I don't know. Nice as it sounds, we've been in each other's faces almost constantly. Here, looking at houses, at my place. It's a lot of togetherness. I'm not sure more togetherness is the answer right this second." Apartness, there was a concept worth investigating. She suspected that giving them both a chance to cool down separately would be better than either of them saying the wrong thing when frustrations were already high.

"All right. Well, call me tonight if you still need to vent."

"You're an angel," Neely said with heartfelt gratitude. "I wouldn't blame you a bit if you started blocking my calls."

"Hey, what are friends for? I was a wreck when I got divorced and you were there for me 24-7. At least wedding stress has a happy ending and I get cake when it's all over. Maybe if they served cake when people signed the divorce papers, it would be less traumatic. Or maybe not."

Once she'd hung up the phone, Neely sat drumming her fingers on her computer keyboard. She was feeling cooped up in this office and eating something might at least lessen her headache. Should she just go alone? Her coworker Amanda had taken a personal day, Leah and Savannah were eating together and Vi was out of the question. Last time Neely had seen her younger sister, Vi had already seemed skittish about having faith in marriages. If the poor girl saw Neely in her current mood, she'd probably end up scarred for life.

* * *

Music pulsed through the speakers, almost a live entity with a heartbeat of its own, weaving between the gyrating dancers on the floor. Colored spotlights flashed red, then green, then blue, casting everyone's skin in unreal hues. It reminded Vi of an alien bar she and an old boyfriend had seen in a sci-fi movie.

Tonight, she was without a boyfriend or even a current lover. Her siblings really had her thinking about relationships lately, and she thought she might take some time before dipping her toe in the water again. Of course, that didn't mean she couldn't at least admire what the dance floor had to offer.

As one of her girlfriends laughed encouragement, Vi danced with a sexy man who had joined their group during the last set of songs. She rolled her hips, letting her body brush his. Outside of where she waitressed, she hadn't been to a club in a while and this was the perfect way to let off some steam after the tough philosophy exam she'd taken today.

When the song was over, Vi and her friends clapped their hands and shouted their appreciation while the deejay announced he'd be taking a little break. Preprogrammed dance music piped through the speakers.

The hottie she'd been gyrating with flashed Vi a smile. "Buy you a drink?"

"Thank you, but no. I'll get my own."

He nodded, unbothered by her refusal and moved through the crowd, undoubtedly off to find a more willing partner. *Would that all male-female relationships were so easy.*

"Uh-oh," her friend Doreen said near Vi's ear, barely audible over the music.

"Problem?" Vi asked.

"You tell me. I think I just saw Brendan on the edge of the floor. Isn't he someone you met here and dated until recently?"

"I think *dating's* probably too strong a word. We went out a few times and then I explained to him how busy my schedule was. He took it pretty well." The disappointment had been in his voice, but he hadn't argued or borne her any ill will. "He's a great guy, though, if you're interested."

Her friend cast another glance his way, considering. "He is cute. It wouldn't be too weird?"

"I'm telling you, we were never that serious."

"Then why don't you make yourself scarce and I'll see if I can generate some small talk."

"Sure, I could use an ice water anyway." Vi shimmied her way through the packed clubgoers, dehydrated but energized. Dancing was about the most fun workout you could have while still fully clothed.

As she was almost at the bar, a man turned away with his own drinks and banged into her. A cold beverage sloshed down her cleavage even as the beer smell hit her.

"I am so sorry," the man said, his gaze shooting upward...and hardening immediately. "You again."

It was Matt, Brendan's friend, and from his expression, he was suddenly less apologetic about dumping his drink on her. Still, he turned behind him and grabbed a handful of white square napkins, thrusting them toward her. "Here."

"Thanks." She dabbed at her chilled skin, wondering if it would damage the fabric if she held her shirt under the heat of an automatic hand-dryer in the women's restroom. "I guess Brendan told you we broke up."

"That you had no more use for him, yeah."

A needlessly harsh way to look at it, but being loyal to his friend was Matt's prerogative. Except that she got the impression he hadn't thought much of her the night they'd met over darts, either.

"You don't like me much, do you?"

He shrugged. "The beer wasn't on purpose, if that's what you mean."

"It wasn't."

"Well, then I think it's egocentric of you to think I have an opinion one way or another. I barely know you. But my guess is, you're used to getting attention even from total strangers." He glanced meaningfully toward the electric-blue blouse that knotted right below her bustline and hung in silky shirttails.

"If I look like a wet T-shirt contestant, that would be *your* fault, bub. And I don't go out of my way to get attention."

"So bumping and grinding on the dance floor and cracking up a class with shocking little asides are just you being you?"

She glared. Neither a yes nor a no would sound good here, not that she owed him an answer. "Brendan is a sweet guy, so I'm sorry if I hurt him by explaining I wasn't looking for a serious relationship. But if not dating him means no more time in your company, well, there was a bullet dodged. You're really an uptight, judgmental jerk, aren't you?"

"Just expressing an honest opinion."

That last comment bothered her the most because it actually sounded like something she might say, when taken to task by her mother or Savannah for being rude or outrageous. *I'm not deliberately outrageous to get attention.* That was... pathetic. She'd always considered herself strong and independent.

"If you'll excuse me, I have a shirt to go salvage." She

raked one final scathing glance over the man, then spun on one blocky heel. She truly hoped never to run into the sanctimonious ass again. If she did, she at least hoped *she* was the one carrying the beer next time.

"Hey, you look upset. What's the matter, kid?" Douglas pushed the door wide and ushered her into his posh bachelor pad, where he pulled her into a comforting embrace.

Vi sniffled. Her big brother gave the *best* hugs. She was glad she'd shelled out the extra cash for the cabbie to bring her here instead of back to her place.

"Nothing serious," she mumbled against Douglas's GSU College of Law sweatshirt. "A dumb guy."

"You want I should break his legs?" Douglas muttered out of the side of his mouth in possibly the worst tough-guy voice ever.

She laughed. "Please. You'd freak if you got blood on one of your suits."

"It's not as if I don't own more casual attire." He gestured at what he was currently wearing. "But you're right, physical violence isn't my thing—I was always more a lover than a fighter. Anything we can sue him for?"

"Emotional distress?" Her laugh was hollow, distantly related to a sob.

"Come tell your big brother all about it." He steered her toward the leather couch.

"I don't even know what to tell." She wasn't upset about Matt. He was a stranger, and what little she did know of him, she didn't like. His words, however, had lingered even after Vi had shrugged back into her mostly dry shirt and told her friends she was going to call it an early night. In Vi's experience, some of the most stinging comments a person could sling at you were the truth. Had there been some honesty in Matt's insults?

And if so, was she really such a blatantly self-centered person that someone who didn't even know her could spot it a mile away?

"Doug, I'm not…awful, am I? I mean, I know Mom acts like she should regularly pray for my soul, but—"

"Of course you're not awful. You're just you."

Somehow, that was the worst thing he could have said right then, and uncharacteristic tears welled up in her eyes. "That's what I was afraid of."

"Oh, damn. I didn't mean to make you cry." He disappeared, then returned with a roll of toilet paper. "Sorry, I don't have a box of tissue. I figured at least this was softer than a paper towel. Come to think of it, I'm not sure I have any of those, either."

She blew her nose loudly.

"Wish I had some ice cream," he said. "That's what always makes my wife feel better."

"You mean your ex-wife?"

"Isn't that what I said?" He sat next to her. "Did you have a fight, break up? I didn't know you were seeing anyone."

"I wasn't really."

"But this guy did something to you!"

"Spilled a beer on a new shirt." Put like that, it didn't sound very earth-shattering.

"Well, that explains the smell. Whatever's wrong, Vi, we'll fix it."

"There's nothing to fix. That's not why I'm here."

"So, why are you? Not that I mind. My DVD collection is your DVD collection. Help yourself to anything in the fridge. I think I have a few Heineken beers and a box of baking soda. I just want to help."

She leaned her head back against the couch and turned to face him. "Amp down—"

"Amp what?"

"Stop stressing. You don't really have to *do* anything, just listen."

"Listen, right."

She knew most guys were more about the taking action and getting results than talking out a problem, but she was surprised Douglas fit that particular masculine stereotype. Had three sisters taught him nothing? "I thought you had a way with the ladies— doesn't that include being a charming companion and listening closely?"

"Kid, nothing about my famed way with the ladies would be appropriate where you are concerned."

"What about Zoe? Didn't you guys talk to each other about bad days at work or a fight with a family member?"

At the mention of his ex-wife, his expression clouded, and Vi regretted saying anything.

"Maybe if I'd been a better listener, she'd still be here." He stared into space. "Or maybe not. Sometimes two people really have no business in a relationship together."

At least he'd tried. Would Vi even get that close to love? Part of her craved it—so bad that she wondered if she did go out of her way to seek attention—but most of her was afraid of it. Lately, all this stuff with Neely's wedding had got her thinking. Would she ever meet a man who wanted to stay with her? If she did, it was hard to believe she'd deserve him. She could be not very nice at times.

"Aw, Douglas, my life is a mess. You're *sure* you don't have any ice cream?"

He stood, holding out his hand. "*That* I can fix.

There's a corner store that has a freezer section and should be open. If you want, I can drive you home, too."

She thought about the classes she had in the morning and concluded there wasn't anything she couldn't blow off just this once. Despite what some might think—and Uncle Darnell called her "flakier than a homemade biscuit"—she was a responsible student. Her attendance was nearly perfect, so she could afford to skip a day.

"Actually, could I crash here? I'll find my own way home tomorrow, but I don't want to go home yet."

Douglas's eyes narrowed. "This guy who has you in unprecedented tears isn't stalking you, is he? Just because I might not be able to personally kick his ass doesn't mean I won't get the problem taken care of—"

She burst out laughing. "God, no. Nothing like that. Just some jerk I barely know said some insulting things to me at a club."

"That's all? I don't get it. Why do you care what some idiot says?"

Silence filled the room as she couldn't bring herself to give the answer. "Because I think maybe he's right." It had been easier in the past to respect herself, to feel superior despite her mistakes and lack of successful relationships, because she hadn't entirely respected her sisters. Why should she be more like Savannah who was Stepford perfect and out of touch with reality, or Neely, who seemed as emotionally accessible as a tray of ice cubes? But this month, she'd seen a warmer side of Neely and a more vulnerable, practical side of Savannah. In comparison, she seemed shallow and aimless. And hungry for the spotlight she'd only ever earned at home by acting out in a juvenile fashion.

Perhaps that was understandable…for a six-year-old.

Douglas glanced toward his room, as if trying to give her a moment to regain her composure. "If you're going to be staying the night, I can grab you a blanket and a shirt of mine. You might feel a little exposed wearing that into the mini-mart, anyway."

"You really think so?" In a few months, it would be summer and women all over the state would be gardening and going through fast-food drive-throughs in their bikini tops. This was just a cute short-sleeved shirt that happened to show a good bit of her stomach.

"Well, Vi it is…I don't know."

"If I were some woman you didn't know, an attractive woman not your sister, what would you think?"

"Nothing I want the old guy working the cash register thinking."

"Douglas, I'm serious."

"So was I. But you've never asked my fashion advice before."

Why had Matt's words struck so deeply? Maybe she was just tired of everyone being disappointed and critical. While she wouldn't have said she needed her family's approval to be happy, the last two outings with Savannah and Neely, their genuine affection toward her, had been nice.

"Vi, honey, I wasn't trying to upset you. I know you've already had a shitty night. I just thought you might be cold going out like that at this hour."

She grinned at the chivalrous attempt—this must be the charming side of him the ladies liked. "No you didn't. You just didn't want to go out with your kid sister showing cleavage. But it's okay. I'll take the shirt."

"Thanks for humoring me."

Huh. She'd actually done it—subdued herself to appease a family member, the kind of personal surrender she'd always sworn against. But she didn't feel like a conformist sell-out or a spineless wimp changing herself to get someone else's sanction. Mostly, she just felt glad she had a big brother who understood the value of post-traumatic ice cream and loved her.

CHAPTER 14

Neely normally went into large family gatherings with a fair amount of trepidation, but this particular Sunday afternoon was different. Tomorrow was the closing on the house and while she and Robert were both happy—and would be overjoyed when it was over—the stress of the past month had made it a quiet car ride to her parents' house. It was as if neither of them was entirely comfortable saying anything for fear of shattering the fragile truce they'd established. The best times were at night. It seemed they were often too drained to make love over the past week, but they still held each other close. Safe in that space where no one had to say anything, they drifted to sleep in each other's arms.

"Remind me again," Robert said suddenly. "Which one is Carol and which one is Josephine?"

"Carol is my mom's youngest sister, married to

Vernon, a practical joker who I will just apologize for in advance, and they have five kids, including triplets. Aunt Jo is the middle sister. She and Darnell have a couple of kids, all grown. Only my cousin Phoebe still lives in-state and will be here today. You'll meet everyone else at the wedding. Leah you know, and there will be a few friends of my parents', but no one will expect you to keep them all straight. Sometimes I can't, and I've known them my whole life." Her relatives often seemed as plentiful—and unstoppable— as kudzu, the transplanted vine that grew over everything in its path.

"Thanks for not minding that I invited Stuart and Bryan," he said.

"No, you should have invited them! I'm sorry more of your friends from the pool league couldn't come. Or even friends of your parents…" She trailed off, remembering that this was exactly why they hadn't been talking much—she'd unintentionally blundered into a sore subject. It turned out Mr. Walsh and his pinochle partner, Mr. Bransen, had a tournament scheduled for today. So Gwen and Everett were going to "pop in for a quick appearance, then dash," as Gwen had put it on the phone.

Though Robert had told them he understood the prior engagement, it was obvious he'd hoped his parents would make this engagement party, casual though it was, a greater priority. Neely had tried to point out that at least they were coming for a little while. In fact, limiting their initial Mason exposure to small doses might be good.

Vi spotted them first, waving from the front porch. After that a crowd gathered, watching them approach.

"I feel like I'm leading a parade," Robert told Neely as they walked from the curb to the house, through the overgrown verdant lawn. "A really, really short one."

Beth met them at the bottom of the porch steps. "The guests of honor! Your father's out back with Douglas and Vernon getting the grill started. I just pray they don't blow up the whole place. Savannah's in the kitchen tossing a salad and Jo's taking antihistamine, but everyone else is up here. Phoebe said she would have bought a gift, but no one's told her where you're registered yet. You *are* registered?"

Neely blinked. They already owned more stuff between the two of them than they could fit into the house. What they needed was a rummage sale, not a gravy boat they'd never use. Good luck explaining that to Beth, who considered gravy a food group.

"Not yet," Robert answered for both of them. "We thought we'd wait until we move in, really get a feel for the new place and what we might need there."

Smooth. A complete and total bold-faced lie, but impressive.

"Oh. Well, that does make sense." Beth nodded approvingly. "Cornelia, this is one smart man. Ready to show him off?"

Rober was good-natured enough not to complain that she made him sound like livestock on display. On the porch, both of Neely's aunts fussed over him as if he were a conquering hero. Or at least the mythic figure who'd broken the "doomed to cat lady" curse. Darnell was less effusive, but offered a hearty handshake, then kissed Neely's cheek.

"How've you been?" she asked, genuinely concerned with his health, but hoping this wasn't one of those times he shared the nitty-gritty of his medical ordeals.

"Never better. Docs say my cholesterol is down and everything looks good, so I've even been allowed to help out at the store. We're busier than a one-legged man in a butt-kickin' contest." Darnell, who was part owner of a printing place that customized coffee mugs, mouse pads, T-shirts and other items, jerked his thumb toward Trent. "We're talking about taking this one on as summer help so he can save up some money before college."

"Hey, Aunt Neely." Her nephew hugged her. "Mom told me you wanted me to be an usher at the wedding. Cool."

Vi appeared at Neely's side, waiting until Darnell and Trent had turned their attention to Robert to nudge her with an elbow.

"Just so you know," Vi whispered, "Mom put me on Phoebe duty, so there shouldn't be any scenes in front of your in-laws."

"Thank you." Neely turned toward her sister, doing a double take. Approaching, she'd noticed Vi's shock of blond hair and red sundress, but hadn't really taken in details. The calf-length dress with its modest scoop neck almost seemed like something Savannah would wear. But the scrolling Celtic knot pattern on the material and large matching gold earrings were more Vi's style. "You look pretty."

Before Vi could respond, Jason joined them, telling Neely it was good to see her again. "It's great your parents had the get-together this weekend. Trent leaves next Saturday for a week at UNC to take the lay of the land, check out the housing options."

Neely shook her head at the thought of the boy going off to college. "Blows my mind how fast he's grown."

"*Yours?*" Jason laughed. "I'm trying to figure out how the scrawny kid I taught to throw a ball is now taller than I am."

"So this must be Robert?" Phoebe approached with a friendly smile. She was wearing white jeans and one of those T-shirts Darnell had printed up for the family reunion each summer: MASON, as Southern as the jar with the same name.

Neely nodded. "Yep, this is Robert Walsh. Robert, my cousin Phoebe Granger."

"Nice to meet you," Robert said, shaking her hand.

Convinced that Robert could hold his own for a few minutes, Neely excused herself to help in the kitchen. Mostly, she wanted to see Savannah. Jason's expression had held no hint of tension, so maybe whatever problems lurked below the surface of their marriage had drifted away.

She came to a halt in the doorway of her mother's kitchen. "Savannah?"

"Hey, there." The woman who'd been swishing her hips to the music from their mother's window radio flashed an embarrassed smile over her shoulder. "You sneaked up on me—thought they'd have you and Robert cornered outside longer. I was headed to say hi as soon as I finished this salad for Mama."

"That's okay. I just thought maybe I could help. As long as it involved washing something or handing it to you and no actual cooking." Everything here, though, seemed well under control. A teapot was burbling on the stove, and containers of beloved family recipes lined the counters. "Wow, I don't think

I've ever seen so many pies and brownies outside of a bakery. Think Carol and Jo went overboard?"

Savannah fidgeted, shifting her weight from one foot to another in a pair of high-heeled sandals. "Actually, *I* brought all the desserts. Except for Aunt Jo's snicker-doodles."

"Oh. They look great, but you didn't have to go to so much trouble."

Her sister shrugged, sending the big, loose curls that brushed her shoulders into bouncy motion. "I've been on a baking binge all week, so the barbecue just gave me a healthy outlet. Prevents me from downing all those calories myself."

As if Savannah had ever gone back for double desserts in her life! Her discipline, however, had paid off. Beneath the hem of her soft denim skirt were smooth shapely legs that attested to years of aerobics, spinning classes and neighborhood walking clubs.

"It's not just the food that looks good," Neely added honestly. "You look great. I like your hair that way."

"Thanks," Savannah mumbled, her normal graciousness replaced with a self-conscious, downcast gaze. "It occurred to me that those curlers were a waste of money and space if I never used them. I'm not sure Jason particularly likes a different look, though."

Neely's heart sank at the flat note in her sister's tone. "I take it the two of you—"

"But I've decided not to let it bother me," Savannah continued. "Before, I was practically invisible to him anyway. At least now I feel good about myself."

"Oh, Savannah. I—"

"Don't. This day is for you, darlin', and you shouldn't spend it worried about us. I'm sure everything will work itself out eventually."

"Absolutely!" She didn't know anyone who made a better wife than Savannah.

"And if not, maybe your friend Leah can recommend a good attorney."

Neely blanched.

"That was supposed to be a joke."

"It wasn't funny." Since there was nothing that required her immediate assistance, Neely turned to go. Then stopped. "You wouldn't want Leah's attorney anyway. She got royally screwed in the divorce." Even voicing the warning made her feel queasy. It was unthinkable Savannah would ever need a lawyer for that. *If it's so unthinkable, why do you have an appointment to sit down next week with Robert and both of your lawyers to discuss the prenuptial agreement?*

Neely had made it as far as the front parlor when her mother bustled through on her way to the kitchen.

"Might want to get out front," Beth instructed. "That's what I was fixin' to tell Savannah. Looks like the Yankees are approaching."

For a minute, Neely imagined her mother had lookouts posted in the trees. Then she decided it was more likely that Robert had seen his parents' car on the road. Still, with her family, she wasn't completely ruling out the rebel scouts.

Neely managed to shoo her relatives inside before the Walshes got out of their car. She would prefer they weren't ambushed right there on the front porch steps. Feeling like a centurion throwing open the doors to the Coliseum, she led them into the house where Beth was crouched in wait.

"Hello, welcome to our home! I'm Elizabeth Mason."

"Gwen and Everett Walsh, nice to meet you." Robert's mother held out the wine they'd brought.

"I'll take that for you," Phoebe offered brightly.

Dutifully sticking to their cousin like white on rice, Vi hip-checked the other woman and retrieved the bottle. "That's okay, I've got it."

Gwen raised her eyebrows as Vi disappeared toward the kitchen, but they were all quickly distracted by the simultaneous arrivals of Leah and Bryan, Robert's pool partner. Other guests followed shortly, most meandering to the backyard, where the smell of smoldering charcoal permeated the spring air. Beth said Douglas had come over early to help arrange the picnic tables, and in the house, Josephine and Savannah set ears of corn to boiling and argued about how to season the homemade potato salad.

Outside Neely caught snatches of conversation, the Walshes asking the Professor about his teaching history and what kind of doctorate he held. He explained that he'd stopped at the Masters level, just as Stuart finished telling Leah, "Long story short, that's the last time *I'll* ever go deep-sea fishing!"

Douglas had handed a cold bottled beer to Bryan as they discussed local bands. Bryan mentioned a group from Hiram with a rock-country sound, and Douglas nodded. "Yeah, they're still pretty obscure, but building loyal fans. My wife plays them in her car incessantly."

My wife? Surprised, Neely turned toward them. She knew divorces took adjustment, but it had been over a year. She would have dismissed it as a meaningless slip of the tongue, but ever since she'd asked Douglas if it would be okay to invite his ex to the wedding and related events, his reaction had nagged at her. He hadn't just given his blessing, he'd seemed…eager.

Before she could decide whether she was imagining things, Robert dropped his arms around her waist, pulling her into a backward hug. "It was nice of your parents to do this for us."

She glanced around at her family—the loud, unruly, nutty bunch of them—and grinned. "Yeah, it was."

"Help me snag Stuart," he said. "My parents are going to leave soon, and I'd like them to meet him."

"They've never met?" Stuart had been his best friend for over twenty years.

Robert's lips thinned. "Well, my parents have been busy."

The two of them circled Stuart over to where his mother sat at an umbrella-shaded table. She was flanked by Carol and Beth, who had just poured three glasses of peach-flavored iced tea.

Mrs. Walsh's eyes widened when she took a sip, but she quickly smiled away her grimace after she swallowed. "My, that is sweet. You folks sure know how to keep dentists in steady business."

Carol laughed, sliding over to make room for Mr. Walsh. The man set a plate of fruit salad on the table as he negotiated his cane and the bench.

Robert used the break in conversation to make introductions. "Mom, Dad, this is Stuart."

Gwen shook hands with the big bear of a man. "Finally! We've heard all about you."

"Same goes, ma'am. I was glad I got a chance to meet you. Rob says you're headed out soon for a big card game? Only cards I was ever good at was Texas Hold 'Em."

"*How* soon?" Beth asked, looking distraught. "We haven't even eaten. I know you have plans, but you've got to stay long enough for food!"

"Afraid we can't," Everett said. "Our loss, I'm sure. This fruit salad's delicious."

Carol snapped her fingers. "Speaking of fruit, Beth, I meant to tell you the farmer's market on Granada is having a huge produce sale this week! We should go. And, Neely, while I'm thinking about it, I clipped these for you." Aunt Carol dug a business-size envelope out of her purse.

Neely found her consideration mostly endearing, but her mother looked ready to kill when Carol added, "Beth, I left some coupons for that new hemorrhoid cream on your mantel. You should really try it with the problems they've been giving you lately."

Beth ground her teeth, and Neely wondered what bothered her mom more—mention of hemorrhoids in front of Robert's parents or the implication that anyone in the Mason family might not be able to afford something without coupons and sales.

"Cornelia, come help me put plates together for Mr. and Mrs. Walsh." She turned back to her guests. "If you're going to leave unfed, it won't be empty-handed. Savannah baked enough pies for a group twice this size. You must take one with you."

Neely dutifully accompanied her mom into the house. Working as a team, the women in the kitchen quickly put together foil pie plates full of food—mostly side dishes and vegetables, since Neely's dad hadn't started the meat yet.

"Check the refrigerator," Beth ordered. "We had fried chicken for dinner last night, and I'm sure there were leftovers. Throw some cold legs into these plates."

No one left the Mason house without eating a hearty meal, taking food with them or possibly both. It was not only a point of personal pride, it was practically a county mandate. On their way back out, Neely almost tripped on the bottom step—distracted by a couple standing near a stately dogwood. Zoe and Douglas. While they weren't embracing, they stood much closer than one might expect from two ex-spouses.

Luckily, Beth didn't notice, as she was more worried about the food. "Oh, for the love of… Let me carry that. It's bad enough the Yankees aren't staying for lunch, let's not dump their food on the back lawn."

Neely relinquished the plate without comment, content to follow her mother back to where the Yan—

er, Walshes sat. It quickly proved to be a good thing she wasn't carrying a plate since she nearly collided with Vi.

"Sorry," her sister said. "I was trying to catch up to Phoebe. God knows how, but she managed to get a hold of a contraband wine cooler. I was trying to keep her distracted so she didn't end up with a second one."

Neely laughed. "Well, we don't have to worry about her impression on Mr. and Mrs. Walsh. They're leaving."

"Oh. You said they weren't staying long, but I didn't realize their visit would be over this soon." Vi scanned the yard, looking for her cousin even though she'd been relieved from duty. "I still don't know how she sneaked a drink past me."

"Hard to separate people from their vices, I guess." Her gaze darted involuntarily to where Zoe and Douglas stood in the distance. Most people would instinctively leave them alone, hoping not to walk in on an awkward moment between the divorced couple, but judging by Zoe's low peal of laughter, awkwardness was not a problem.

Vi watched, too. "I'm worried about him."

"At least they had an amicable split."

"No, they didn't. They fought like cats and dogs—it's just that they're too good at the making-up part to remember why they broke up. I applaud Zoe's passionate nature and worthy causes, but you know she drives

Douglas nuts with all of it. And even though he says he supports her, how long before he starts blowing things off and trying to charm his way out of it? The only things he ever took seriously were the bar exam and Zoe, but even that turned out to be dysfunctional."

"He's been dating an awful lot, though," Neely pointed out. "Isn't that a sign that he's moved on?"

"Or a sign that he's trying to force it because he's having trouble letting go. Just a hunch."

In general, Neely preferred facts and figures to nebulous hunches, but Vi had always been close to Douglas. "Maybe you're right."

"Really? I expected you to say I was overreacting. You agreeing with me could be a serious blow to my reputation as the family flake."

"You're not a flake. You just make some…unique choices. I was listening to Dad earlier telling the Walshes about how he fell into teaching and it made me think of you." Just because Vi hadn't figured out her way yet didn't mean she wouldn't. "He had his Master's in history, but considered all his civil war interest a hobby, not a career. He didn't know what he wanted to do and was talking about maybe going back to school again. It was Mom who suggested any return be as a teacher, not a student."

"Sounds like Mom, bossing other people around."

They both knew their father had loved being a professor; Vi was just taking a verbal swipe at Beth.

Smothering a grin, Neely made her own swipe. "Don't think of it as bossing, think of it as the love of a good woman showing him the way. Maybe all you need is a good man to take you in hand."

"First man who tries to take me 'in hand' will draw back a bloody stump. I—oh, Mrs. Walsh."

Gwen glanced from Vi to Neely. "We were just coming to say goodbye, dear. If we don't leave now, Everett could risk losing his place in the tournament."

"I wish you could stay, but thank you for coming."

"Of course. It was—" Gwen floundered a moment before smiling brightly. "Thanks for having us!"

Neely hugged them both, then watched Robert walk them to their car. From the slump of his shoulders, she could see his mood visibly sink as they drove away. Coming from a sane family must not be perfect, either. For all the times Beth had exasperated her or Vi had embarrassed her, Neely always knew her family loved her. Maybe she'd taken that for granted in the past, but it wasn't too late to learn from her mistakes and change her future.

Savannah carried what was left of one sheet cake toward the house, already planning how she could tweak the recipe for a future event. People had insisted after lunch that they were too stuffed to enjoy the desserts, but once she'd cajoled a few of them into trying a bite, her cake, pies and walnut brownies had disappeared quickly.

When she'd started taking trays to the car this morning, Jason had watched from the kitchen table with a lifted eyebrow. "I know you want to help your sister, and I'm sure she appreciates it, but she wouldn't have wanted you to work your fingers to the bone over it. Other people will be bringing food, too, right?"

Funny that someone so worried that she was overworked hadn't offered to help her carry anything, but she hadn't commented as he returned to his newspaper. Truthfully, she hadn't minded the baking. It had soothed her all week as she thought about Trent's upcoming spring break trip. When both the boys were in high school, she'd always thought it would be hardest when Adam went to college, because he was the first. Now, she realized it would actually be harder when Trent moved out because he was the last.

In addition to the other baked goods, there had been two dozen cookies, but Trent's study group Friday night had demolished those almost before they'd cooled. It was hard to begrudge them the snacks when she'd heard one boy in the living room pause midrave about the car his father was getting him for graduation to say, "Your mom made these herself? They're freaking awesome."

Trent had laughed, and even from the next room she'd caught the pride in his voice. "Now you know why our school bake sales always do so well. Speaking of which, I hear we made enough to get that band for the prom…."

Jason might no longer need her help studying for the written portions of medical exams and Trent had long since been able to tie his own shoes, but all people needed to eat.

"Excuse me, fellas." She walked between Robert and his friend, who were chatting on the back porch steps. Neely wasn't with them—last Savannah had seen, her sister had been helping Leah politely decline a job working for Uncle Darnell.

Robert's friend hopped up as she passed. "Here, let me get that for you, ma'am." He opened the door for her as Robert said he'd go grab a couple more beers.

"Thank you…" She searched her memory bank for the man's name, knowing she'd caught it when he first arrived several hours ago. "Bryan."

"I'm impressed." He followed her inside. "Whenever I meet more than one or two people together, I have a devil of a time getting all the names straight."

"I've had lots of cocktail party and charity dinner practice," she said, setting the cake on her mom's kitchen counter. "I'm Sa—"

"Savannah, right?"

She laughed. "Thought you had trouble with names."

"I make exceptions for pretty ladies," he teased. "Actually, Robert and I were just talking about you. He said you made most of this food. Wow. Do you cater professionally?"

Her, a professional? "Not even close."

"That's a shame. I wanted to see about ordering a cake for my daughter's birthday next weekend—it'll be the first year she's actually with me on the big day since the divorce. But I can go through a grocery store. Eight-year-olds aren't picky." He sighed and Savannah could see the time he wished he was spending with his little girl in his expression. "It's just that you want the best for your kids, you know?"

Did she ever. "Hey, just because I don't do this for a living doesn't mean I wouldn't be willing to do a favor for a friend of Robert's, especially one who has an eight-year-old daughter! I had boys and recently found instructions for a cake that comes out looking like a princess castle that is just too adorable. I haven't had a good excuse to make it."

As Savannah rinsed dishes, Bryan sat on the step

stool her mother kept nearby to reach the cabinet with the spare lightbulbs and pickling jars. He told her all about his daughter, Mel, and his plans for her birthday. By the time Jason came looking for Savannah, Bryan was helping her dry glasses as she shared some of her favorite anecdotes about the boys when they were Mel's age.

"Savannah, are you—" Her husband drew up short, cocking his head to the side.

She waited for him to finish his sentence, then prompted him. "Did Mama need me to brew more tea?"

"What? No. I think she has plenty. I was looking for you because Trent's ready to go, and I should get some rest. I'll probably be at the hospital tonight."

"Oh. All right, then, just let me get my purse. I can say goodbye to everyone outside." She glanced from her husband to the other man. "Have you met Bryan, Robert's pool partner?"

Jason nodded curtly. "Earlier."

"Bryan, I'll talk to you later this week?"

He nodded, patting the front pocket of his jeans. "Got your number right here, thanks. I know Mel will be ecstatic."

Savannah turned toward the front parlor, where she was sure she'd left her purse. The back door banged shut as Bryan rejoined what remained of the crowd outside.

"Do you know him?" Jason asked.

"Bryan? I met him today, same as you."

"And you gave him your phone number?"

She laughed. "Lots of people have our phone number."

"I'm sorry I don't find my wife handing out her number to strange men all that amusing."

Part of her was unexpectedly flattered that her husband, who seemed in his own world lately—one that only peripherally included her—sounded so possessive. The rest of her was just plain irked. "I did PTA board for years, football boosters for Trent and Adam. I exchange my number with fathers all the time. Bryan just wants my help with his little girl's birthday party. It's the first he's planned as a single father."

Jason grunted. "So he's not married?"

There was her purse, sitting between the wall and her mother's favorite rocker. Savannah yanked the shoulder bag strap up her arm and turned to glare at her husband. "You can't honestly be jealous?"

"Of course not. It's just that there are certain things that aren't always appropriate. And…I didn't like the way he looked at you."

"You saw us together for all of three seconds," she said as she walked past him. Maybe she was tired of worrying so much about what was appropriate. Not that she planned to do anything wrong, but if someone thought her having a pleasant conversation in her mother's kitchen with a fellow parent was scandalous, they could just get stuffed.

"Savannah, wait. I don't know why I'm overreacting. I just don't understand what's been wrong with you lately, and I guess I—"

"Wrong! With *me*?" What was it he took issue with? The perfectly folded laundry, the being patient when he came home hours later than he'd estimated, the getting up early so that her makeup was on and breakfast fixed when everyone else rolled out of bed? Yeah, she was a nightmare of a wife.

"You have to admit, you've been unpredictable," he said. "Moodier, wearing different clothes."

"What, exactly, is the problem with my clothes?"

He eyed her warily. "Nothing, exactly. But they are different. Babe, I know you're going through some changes right now, I see it in a lot of my patients, and—"

She pressed a single finger to his lips. "If you say one word about hormones, you'll be cooking your own meals for the next twenty years."

"*See?*" He brushed her finger away. "This is what I mean. Since when do you threaten anyone? You've always been…"

Loving, accommodating, soft-spoken. *Invisible.* Maybe she'd just flat-out become boring and that was why he'd stopped noticing her. Like pretty wallpaper that you love when you pick it out, but day after day, you cease to really see it. Why should you?

"Jason." She didn't want to fight, had never been a fan of conflict, but she didn't want to revert to how everything had been the last few months, either. "You'd be doing us both a favor if you don't dwell on how I've 'always' been. Honestly, I haven't been one hundred percent happy lately, and it's my responsibility to fix that. So expect changes."

His gaze was troubled, his brow pinched into the frown he'd worn the few times the boys had come home with bad grades. "What kind of changes?"

She shrugged. "Nothing major. Or, I don't know, maybe something that is major. Whatever's necessary."

"Mom, Dad?" Trent walked into the room jangling the keys. His parents had promised he could drive home. "I thought we were leaving. You ready?"

I am, Savannah thought. *I really am.*

Over the years, she'd made a concerted effort not to bother Jason with trivial problems. When he came home after an emergency delivery that had left both mother and baby in critical condition, the last thing he wanted to hear about was how the cable guy hadn't bothered to show up when he promised or the occasionally petty hierarchy of neighborhood housewives—that Sue Ellen Schramm was always stirring up trouble. In general, Savannah had been raised to believe complaining wasn't very ladylike. So even though she'd put it as gently as she could, her being able to tell him she was unhappy was a major milestone.

It felt liberating, no matter how much he'd scowled at her. *Well, you know what they say. Admitting you have a problem is the first step.*

Now she was anxious to take the next ones and see where they led.

CHAPTER 15

Leaning against a picnic table, Neely watched her dad scrape the grill. "Thanks for cooking, everything was great."

"Happy to help. It was a pretty enjoyable shindig."

He had seemed to have a good time. She'd heard her quiet father talk more today than in the past year. This was also the first time in a long while she could remember having a few minutes alone with him. Robert and Beth were carrying dishes inside, and Vi was trying to round up Douglas so that he could say goodbye before Robert and Neely left. Just about everyone else had gone home.

"Anything I can do to help, Dad?"

"Hmm?" The Professor shook his head. "That's all right. Nothing much more here that needs to be done, if you'd like to go in."

"Actually, I was thinking it was kind of nice to hang out with you." Earlier, when she'd been reminded how close Vi and Douglas were, she'd thought it might be nice to have a man she could talk to sometimes. Maybe the Professor wouldn't have a lot to say, but he certainly seemed like a good listener.

"Something on your mind, Cornelia?"

"No. Yes. Getting married, I suppose."

Her father nodded. "Big step. It's to be expected that you'd be thinking a lot about it as the big day approaches. Sometimes I think if more people gave it more honest consideration, they could save themselves some heartbreak later."

Neely couldn't see the street from the back, but not for the first time she wondered if Zoe had left already or was still here somewhere. "Divorce happens for all kinds of reasons, though."

"True."

An early-evening breeze rippled over her arms and she wished she had a jacket with her. Or Robert to hold her close. "Did you and Mom ever…have problems?"

He rocked back on his heels. "Every marriage has problems, sweet pea. Don't worry about being a perfect wife, because you can't. And don't beat him up over not being perfect, either. Lord knows how your mother's put up with all my absentmindedness, but we never considered parting ways. What would I do without her? She's the heart and soul of this family."

Neely had never heard her father speak so poetically about anything except the Continental Congress. "That's nice to know. Vi…" She stopped herself, not wanting to break a confidence. Still, Neely couldn't help wishing her parents had been more demonstrative with their affection to each other. Maybe Vi wouldn't have secretly worried about their marriage. *And maybe you'd have a better idea of how to open up to people?*

"What about your sister?"

"Nothing. Just, I think that after all of us left home, she perceived you and Mom as being distant with each other sometimes."

"Distant? Let me tell you something about your mother. She might be reserved, like you—"

Beth? *Reserved?* Then again, Neely couldn't remember ever seeing her mother cry, not even when she'd lost her parents. Nor could she remember her mom kissing the Professor where others could see.

"—but she's been the love of my life. Did she tell you that between Douglas and Vidalia, there was one other pregnancy? Lost the baby early on. Somehow, *she* ended up comforting *me* over the miscarriage. We've held on to each other through every tragedy and celebration in fifty years, but you know what? I think that the defining moments of this marriage have been the small day-to-day details. No one but my Elizabeth knows exactly how dark I like my toast or can remember where I left my reading glasses."

Random memories of her parents sped by, like billboards passed on the freeway. Vi would have said their mother ordered the Professor around, nagging him. But from the inside, it seemed as if Beth had merely been taking care of him, which he'd appreciated. Neely admired the marriage they'd built, the way they'd made it last. Not everyone did. Hopefully, she and Robert would find their way.

"Are you *crazy?*" Vi hadn't meant to be so shrill, though the mistake balanced out cosmically. She was sure her brother hadn't meant to be so stupid, either.

"Vi." Douglas sprang away from his ex-wife, whom he'd been kissing up against the side of the house. "We, ah, didn't think we'd be…in anyone's way here."

Didn't think they'd be caught, he meant. What was he, a sixteen-year-old kid making out with his girlfriend? Vi shook her head, not making eye contact with Zoe so that the woman had a moment to compose herself. It wasn't as if Vi was passing judgment—they were consenting adults—but if anyone in the family saw them together like this, certain assumptions would be made. She'd like to know how he would explain to their parents that no, there was no reconciliation, just occasional sex.

"*Mom* sent me to find you. Neely and Robert are leaving soon and wanted to say goodbye." Thank God Beth hadn't come looking herself.

Douglas paled, no doubt thinking the same thing. "Oh. We'll be right in then, thanks."

"Actually—" Zoe interrupted, looking guilty and apologetic "—maybe I should just go. That might be best. Vi, it was nice to see you again. Douglas…" Her hand barely brushed along his cheek before dropping back to her side.

"It's always good to see you," he said, his voice so husky that Vi felt more an intruder than she had when she'd rounded the corner and caught them kissing in the elongated shadows. "Maybe I could call you."

"We've talked about that," his ex-wife said.

"We've talked about this, too."

"I know, and look where we ended up, anyway. That's why I don't think you should call." She ducked under his arm and darted a few steps away, moving with the nimble speed of a deer. "Take care of yourself, Douglas."

He watched her go, and Vi found herself staring at the sky, wishing she hadn't witnessed any of this. Since she had, could she really let it go? It was *his* life, she reminded herself, and she'd never welcomed unsolicited feedback on hers.

Screw that. "Don't do this to yourself, bro. You know you make each other miserable."

"I know."

She took a deep breath. "Then why do you keep falling in this same trap?"

"Maybe I'm not as strong as you or Neely or Savannah would be. Maybe I'm just in love and stupid."

He thought Vi was like her older sisters?

But this wasn't about her. She couldn't help remembering what he'd said in his apartment, about some people having no business together. "If the two of you got back together, really back together, do you think you would make her happy?"

To his credit, he didn't offer one of his glib answers but considered it seriously. "No. Not forever. There are things about us neither can change. Maybe even things that we like about each other in the short run would make living together very difficult."

"Do you want her to be happy?" Vi cared less about Zoe than her big brother, but she suspected this was the way to make her case.

"Yeah. I do." He ran a hand through his already disheveled hair. "Is this where you tell me that if I love her, I should let her go?"

She grinned, hoping to make him do the same, even though she knew how difficult changing habits could be. *Maybe we could both give it a try.* "Nah, clichés are for nerds. I was going to say, if she breaks your heart again, don't come crying to me."

Douglas squeezed her hand, then pulled her in for a hug.

"Actually," she whispered. "You can always come crying to me. I'll even buy the ice cream."

"Softie."

"I didn't promise not to say I told you so or call you a dumb-ass"

"Well. Nobody's perfect."

When the door to Robert's apartment swung open Wednesday afternoon, Neely was already smiling her greeting. It had been a long day at work, and she was really looking forward to seeing him—even if tonight was a designated packing night and didn't leave much time for cuddling and relaxation. The sooner they got all their stuff ready to move, the sooner they could be living in the house they'd closed on two days ago.

We own a home now. The thought still gave her shivers.

"Hi." Robert held a brown cardboard box in each of his hands. "Great, you brought the bubble wrap. Sorry I keep forgetting."

Neely had packed most of her belongings, and

Stuart would be by with his truck that weekend to help them start moving. Robert's apartment was the bigger chore, however. If left up to him, he might have procrastinated indefinitely. Good thing he had her to help him stay organized.

An hour later, she'd reconsidered. It would take divine intervention to keep Robert Walsh organized.

"You're sure you need this?" Neely asked, lifting a box of old report cards, art projects and various ribbons from track-and-field events. She knew parents often kept such things as their children grew, but they were already going to need all the storage space they could maximize in the house. Was it crucial that he held on to a written record of his middle-school geometry grade? The only papers she kept year after year were those related to tax documentation and certain legal policies, such as copies of the lease and her life insurance.

"Well…" Robert reached out and took the box from her, an unmistakably protective gesture. Even if he couldn't provide a logical reason for needing colored pencil sketches he'd done thirty years ago, he clearly didn't want her to toss them.

In fact, he took more than one thing out of her hands and even *unpacked* shoe boxes and other containers to show her the tidbits inside and explain their sentimental value. At this rate, they'd never move into their new house. She tried to assign Robert the simple task of wrapping and packing dishes in the kitchen so that he wasn't hovering, but he kept peeking around the corner to check on her and explain why each and every item deserved a place in their new home.

I give up. "Are you hungry? Maybe we could break for pizza," she suggested.

By the time the pepperoni and green pepper deep dish arrived, they were having a heated debate over Robert's movie collection.

"I just don't understand why you need copies of *Casablanca, The Natural* and *Rocky* on VHS *and* DVD." Those examples were just the tip of the iceberg—half of the films he owned were doubles.

"Because I own a VCR *and* a DVD player," he retorted.

Neely ground her teeth and went to pour them both drinks. An iced beverage might cool her temper. Robert was making her out to be a lunatic because she wouldn't find room in *their* new house for "a few VCR tapes and old school papers." Except his pack-rat tendencies extended far beyond that, and she'd have to find more room than just an empty drawer for videotaped movies he now only watched on DVD. For instance, rather than let acquaintances get rid of "perfectly good computers," Robert bought the PCs cheap with nebulous plans to salvage parts. As a result, the table in his office looked like an IBM graveyard, with motherboards, stereo equipment and different bits of wiring scattered about. It was difficult for Neely to surrender control of her environment and while she anticipated compromise, she wanted some sign that he would meet her halfway. Some sign that he could respect her neatnik tendencies and wouldn't be resenting her two months into the marriage and wishing she was more sentimental like him.

She reached into the refrigerator and pulled out a two-liter bottle of soda. Little boxes on the back of the shelf caught her attention. He'd explained to her the first time she asked that he'd bought some film in bulk once and it kept better in the refrigerator. She'd never questioned that, since Aunt Carol constantly extolled the financial virtues of buying in bulk, but now that she thought about it, she'd only ever seen Robert use a digital camera. Why did he need twelve unused rolls of film?

Curious, she grabbed one to see if there was an expiration date—*1992!* She scooped a handful of them in the trash.

Her fiancé immediately barreled into the small room. "What was that? You threw something away."

He couldn't have sounded more accusatory if he'd charged her with seducing his best friend.

"Just film. It expired years ago." Prior to his even moving into this apartment, by her calculations. He'd packed and brought along expired film? Well, that was before he had her. "Besides, you have a digital camera. I don't think I've ever seen you use a roll of film."

"So you just decided for yourself to throw out something of mine?" he asked. "Maybe we should pitch my digital camera, since you have one, too."

His sarcastic hyperbole stung. "You *know* I wouldn't do that. If I'd run across a container of expired cottage cheese, would you complain about my throwing that out?"

But her pride wasn't the only one pricked now. "You said you wanted to come over to help, but I think we both know what you really wanted was to come over and take charge. Trying to keep me out of my own office to let you pack my things?"

"I am trying to help," she retorted. "But you're being impossible."

"And you're being controlling."

"Robert, if left up to you, when would we get around to packing everything? I'm the one who started the search for real estate agents in the first place and the one making most of the wedding plans. If I never took control, how many things would be left undone?"

"Excuse me for not being more grateful about you walking in here and trying to tell me what parts of my old life I have to get rid of to suit you. Where does it end—you dictating which friends I can keep, when they can drop by?"

She clenched her fists. "When have I *ever* suggested that you should ditch your friends?"

"Out loud? Never. But you don't always look thrilled when Stuart or Sheila drops by."

"I like most of your friends, and even if I didn't, I wouldn't try to keep you from seeing them. You don't think I know that they're as important to you as Leah is to me? They have to adjust, though. Bryan's divorced and Stuart's single, but *you'll* be married. They can't pop in unannounced, interrupting an intimate dinner with a six-pack and news that the game just went into overtime and expect me to be happy."

Robert set his jaw, looking to the side and not saying anything for a long, uncomfortable moment. "I guess Stuart and Bryan aren't the only ones who need to make adjustments, are they?"

She managed a tremulous smile. "I guess not."

* * *

"Thanks for agreeing to meet me," Neely said between breaths. Leah had said she was free midday to join Neely for thirty minutes of power walking at the small park near the office.

"You're welcome." Despite the creeping warmth as the sun rose higher in the cloudless sky, Leah had no visible perspiration and was breathing much easier than her friend. "I got the impression you didn't suggest this just so we could enjoy the lovely spring day?"

No. Though the widely spaced Bradford pear trees along the path were gorgeous, with their full white blooms that would pass too quickly to green leaves, Neely's sudden yen for exercise had stemmed from the trouble she'd had zipping her khaki slacks this morning. Too bad she couldn't just wear her comfortable blue shorts back to work this afternoon. "I must be stress-eating," she confided. "I've gained weight."

"It's not noticeable."

"Maybe not yet, but if I keep going at this rate, I won't be able to wear my wedding dress in two months! So I'm taking a page out of your book and making time for a little physical activity. Besides, you've been telling me that the gym has really helped you work out some frustration. I thought everything would be less tense after the closing earlier this week!"

"The closing was just one hurdle. Don't be too hard on yourself, moving has caused temporary insanity in many a strong person."

Good to know, because she was definitely teetering on the edge. "I went to Robert's last night, ostensibly to pack, but we ended up arguing."

Leah scooted over, letting a more ambitious female jogger pass. "Anything serious?"

"Hard to say. Honestly, I don't know how anyone who's been through one move with her significant other can ever face another. I'd rather spend the rest of our lives in the new house than do this again."

"Well, at least you're still talking about spending the rest of your lives together." Leah smiled. "That's a decent sign. What about after the fight, did you stay the night at his place or go home?"

"Stayed with him." Their mostly silent dinner had been awkward, but she'd stuck it out. Before she'd finally fallen asleep, he had slid his arm over her side, lacing his fingers with hers. "It started with stupid, small stuff and escalated out of proportion. But I ask you, does it make any sense to keep expired film?"

"I'm here to offer a sympathetic ear, not get dragged into this. If I say anything negative about Robert, it can and will be held against me once you guys have made up. Which you absolutely will. He's one of the good ones, Neely."

"I know." Sometimes she thought that was the problem. His flaws all seemed superficial, while she wasn't always so good with the important stuff. He'd been hurt in the past and even now had trouble voicing feelings of discontent to his parents. She wanted to be there for him, but worried about whether or not they'd be a perfect fit.

"I will make one suggestion—the bridal shower is around the corner and Savannah and I promised we'd e-mail the guests as soon as you had a registry somewhere. Why don't you and Robert take time off from the moving plans and go take care of it tonight? Register for silly stuff."

Postponing what needed to be done for yet another night went against Neely's nature. "I don't want my loved ones spending money on stuff we don't need."

"Not silly stuff as in junk you won't use, just items you can both enjoy but never would have bought for yourself. You don't have to be practical all the time, Neely. Have fun, too. Keep reminding yourself that the reason you're marrying this man in the first place is that you make each other *happy*. Don't let all the stupid details get in the way of that."

"You're very wise."

Leah nodded sagely. "I try. Besides dispensing pearls of wisdom, is there more I can do to help? Maybe as maid of honor, I should be shouldering some of this stress."

"Are you kidding? You're already my twenty-four-hour vent hotline, and you and Savannah are planning the bridal shower."

"Don't worry about that. Except for e-mailing updates to the guests, there's not much left to do. Savannah is killer organized—you two definitely came from the same gene pool. Wait until you see the menu she has planned! She was very excited about it, said something about us being a test audience."

This shifted Neely's worries from her love life to her sister's. Maybe Savannah was simply enthusiastic about the shower. On the other hand, if Neely was a stress-eater, her sister had always been a stress-cooker. Neely just hoped both of their relationships were on more even ground before the wedding rolled around.

*

CHAPTER 16

Dinner Friday night was a quiet affair, leaving Savannah without much of an appetite. Trent had driven off with a friend that afternoon and wouldn't be back for nine whole days. Jason was on call tonight, but home long enough to share dinner with his wife. It might have been a more intimate experience if he hadn't brought a novel to the table with him, choosing to finish the last two chapters of a techno-thriller rather than converse.

Not that she knew what she'd say, anyway.

She twirled pasta around her fork, marveling at the irony. More than anything, she wanted to break the mounting silence between her and her husband, so why couldn't she? She felt strangely paralyzed, tongue-tied in his presence, even though there were so many things she wanted to share with him. Then again, he might scoff—either at her missing Trent already or the half-formed plan in the back of her mind about cooking for money. For years, she'd been taking dishes to potlucks and creating the most popular desserts for school and church bake sales only to have people beg for the recipes. Still…Savannah the businesswoman?

Was it really so strange to think she could try her hand at professional catering?

Why not? Look how quickly she'd been able to put together Neely's shower. She had time on her hands, in the calm before Trent's end-of-the-year activities, graduation and relocation to college. But what about women who worked sixty-hour weeks or had small children at home? Some of them might not have the time to pull together a party, baby shower or romantic dinner. She could give them a homemade alternative to picking up something generic at the grocery store.

Could she do it efficiently enough to make it cost-effective, though? It wasn't a professional endeavor if it didn't turn a profit, but she had to keep her prices competitive to—

"Aren't you going to get that?"

Savannah blinked, realizing her husband had spoken. "What?" By the time she'd got the word out, the phone had rung again.

Scowling, she pushed back her chair. Jason could have answered; he lived here, too. Then again, most of the calls *were* for her. The hospital tended to reach him through his pager or cell phone.

"Hello?"

"May I talk to Savannah, please?" a cheerful male voice she didn't recognize asked.

If she were the paranoid type, she'd think telemarketers actually planted cameras in people's homes to see when they were eating and call during dinner. "Speaking."

"Hi, it's Bryan Albright."

A smile spread across her face. "Hey, Bryan. It is so nice to hear from you." He was a welcome respite from someone pitching her carpet cleaning services or satellite television installation. She'd dropped off his daughter's cake yesterday afternoon and had enjoyed chatting with him.

"Mel and her friends are watching a DVD I rented them," he said, "and I won't stay on the phone long. But I had to call and say thanks again. You should have seen her face when she got that cake. I took pictures— I should probably send you one."

"Oh, I'd love that. Do you have my e-mail address?" She waited while he found a pen, then recited it.

"It's too bad you don't do this professionally. More than one parent asked where I bought the cake."

"Really?" Her heart pounded a little faster, excitement warming her. "Because I've been think-ing…maybe I was a little too hasty when I said no before. Nothing's definite yet, but feel free to pass on my phone number, okay?"

"Absolutely! But if you're going to do this profes-sionally, you should let me pay you."

"Nonsense. I told you it was a favor, and I was happy to do it. I might not have pursued this without your encouragement, Bryan."

They hung up soon after, so that he could enjoy his daughter's birthday with her. Savannah replaced the phone in the cradle, humming to herself. She didn't know if she could really get a business off the ground, but the challenge filled her with more happy antici-pation than she'd felt in a long time.

She turned, freezing at the glacial expression in Jason's eyes.

"What?" she asked, noting distantly that she sounded like one of her boys when they were being defensive.

"That was the man from Neely's party? The one who was looking at you?"

Oh, honestly. "You know, Jason, some men enjoy looking at a woman and occasionally even smiling at her." Just because her husband couldn't be bothered to do either didn't mean she had to defend herself against ludicrous jealousy.

Her husband got to his feet. "That's all you have to say? I'm supposed to sit back and let Bryan do whatever it is 'some men' enjoy doing? How would you feel if I were ogling the nurses I work with?"

For all she knew, he was.

The thought struck her horribly in the pit of her stomach. Not because she thought Jason was making time with someone at the clinic, just because they'd become so estranged she wasn't sure she'd know if he were. "Jason, I'm not ogling anyone. You know that, don't you?"

"Yes. I think." He sighed, but his expression remained mutinous. "But you gave this man your phone number, and now he's calling us in the middle of dinner. You also gave him your e-mail address and asked him to pass your number along to others."

"None of which is your concern." Now, why had she said that instead of just explaining her idea about catering? Was it because she still wasn't sure if he'd dismiss it, or was she too angry to do so under these circumstances? When she shared her idea, she didn't want it to be because she was being cross-examined. "That was my phone call."

"How could I not overhear when you were two feet away, chirping into the phone and grinning like a schoolgirl with a crush? You're my wife, Savannah, that makes your life my concern."

"Then maybe you should start taking a more active interest."

He sat back in his chair, as if the unexpected anger in her tone had actually knocked him off balance. It certainly had surprised her.

"Excuse me?" he asked incredulously. "One minute, you're telling me it's none of my concern, and the next you're—"

"I'm sorry." She dropped into the chair next to him. "Maybe I should have talked to you weeks ago. Months. Hell, I don't know, years?"

"Savannah, it's not like you to swear." He looked really nervous now. "Please tell me what's going on."

She lifted the book he'd been reading off the table. "This, for starters. How long has it been since we had the house to ourselves?"

He flushed guiltily but tried to rationalize. "Pretty soon, we'll have lots of time alone together, though."

"Exactly. And it's been…worrying me. What do you think our life will be like then?"

"I'm not sure what to expect." His tone was guarded, making it clear that he wasn't sure what to expect from *her*.

She sighed. "We've really lost touch with each other, haven't we?"

"Maybe," he said stiffly. "I know that a few months ago, I wouldn't have cared if I heard you on the phone being friendly to some guy. You were right about interacting with people from the PTA, the sports groups, even the medical board. I guess it bothers me now because it's paired with so many other changes. You telling me you aren't happy, changing the way you dress...and it's been a long time since we made love, Savannah."

Her laugh was hollow. "And you thought another man might be the cause of that?"

"No. But sometimes wives turn to other men if they're unhappy enough. Not that I think you would," he added quickly. "Not that I don't trust you. I just don't understand."

She supposed that was her fault. She'd worked for so many years to make herself quietly indispensable, working to anticipate his needs before he even realized he needed her that it was no wonder he occasionally took her for granted. "Mostly, I've been happy. We've had a lovely life together, but it's changing. I didn't really want it to, but the boys are growing up and moving on, whether I like it or not. I need to do the same."

"Move on?" Alarm skittered through him, almost a visible entity.

"No!" She covered his hand with hers. "No, change. Grow. I'd like *us* to change. I bought a new refrigerator last year and you barely noticed."

"I trust your judgment. Besides, it's not as if I use the kitchen as much as you do."

"That's not the point! Do you even know when your mother's birthday is, or do you just assume I'll buy her a card? When was the last time *you* went to a parent-teacher conference or decided what Trent's punishment should be if he breaks curfew? I'm your wife, Jason, not your assistant. I don't want to just have your coffee ready in the morning and pick up your dry cleaning and generally make your life easier. Maybe that is what I wanted for a long time, because I wanted so much to be the wife you deserve, but I don't think that's enough anymore. I'm building goals of my own."

Since she'd come this far, the rest of it got easier to say. "A-about the other thing, making love? Not too long ago, I concocted this plan to seduce you after Trent went to bed. But then I, um, overheard you talking to him. I didn't set out to eavesdrop, I was just collecting laundry. You told him he should humor me if I was being clingy, and after that I was afraid you would see any overtures on my part as…needy."

"Oh, Savannah, I'm sorry, babe. I never meant to hurt your feelings. You're not a clingy wife! Truthfully, you aren't a clingy mother, but seventeen-year-old boys often view things differently than their parents."

"Really?" Tears pricked her eyes. "You don't see me as too dependent, without a life of my own?"

He squeezed her fingers. "I don't want you to have a separate life, I want us to repair the one we have together. Can we do that? It can't be too late, not when I love you this much."

"I love you, too."

He leaned across the corner of the table, crushing his mouth to hers. If the conversation had been hesitant and uncertain, his kisses certainly weren't. His tongue slid between her lips, making her knees go as weak now as they had when she was nineteen. *God, I've missed him.* A dam broke inside her, desire and emotion that she'd tried to repress swelling free, overwhelming her.

He pulled away, brushing his thumb over her cheek. "Please don't cry. Have I really been that bad a husband?"

"No. We've had some really great years together."

He cupped her face, leaning in for another kiss. "Let's figure out how to have a whole bunch more."

* * *

Robert met Neely in the parking garage. His kiss hello was affectionate, but his expression was wary as he asked, "So back over to my place to pack up the last few boxes?"

She opened her mouth, but the intended yes was lodged in her throat. Leah's words from a few days ago came back to her, about taking time out of all the wedding and moving madness to remember *why* they were getting married and living together. "What if I buy you dinner first? Rio Bueno?"

He raised his eyebrows. "Well, you know I've never turned that down."

Their favorite Mexican restaurant was low-key, which suited Neely. She knew of some cantinas that boasted bright, colorful decorations and mariachi bands that wandered through the room entertaining diners. But Rio Bueno was understated, letting the food create all the ambience needed to bring back patrons. Neely breathed in the familiar scents and spices, nodding to the hostess, who knew them by name.

As soon as they were seated, Robert picked up the menu, and Neely laughed.

"Don't you have that thing memorized already?"

He waggled his eyebrows at her as she took a seat. "I like looking at the pictures to get me in the mood."

"Pervert."

He paused, then flashed her a slow smile. "Bet I can change your mind by the end of the night."

She feigned shock. "I was thinking about getting a margarita, but now I see I need to keep my wits about me so you don't take advantage."

"Wits are overrated. Why not order us a pitcher?"

"Okay, but you're driving home."

Dinner was fun. They teased each other the same way they had when they'd first become lovers, and being pointlessly silly was a nice change of pace. This was the first night in weeks where she'd felt free-spirited, not overwhelmed by family commitments, or the house closing or wedding plans.

"Leah is a smart lady," she muttered.

Robert swallowed a bite of enchilada. "Pardon me?"

"Oh. I was…Leah suggested that maybe we needed a night out, away from all the recent stress."

He straightened. "I guess it has been pretty, er, stressful."

"Am I driving you crazy?" she asked bluntly, unable to help herself. They'd been arguing so often and making love so rarely. Was she being too much of a nag? Would another woman be more under-standing about his prenuptial jitters and private space? Was he dragging his feet because he was a disorganized procrastinator by nature, or because he was having doubts?

"No crazier than I'm driving you," he admitted. "You're not having second thoughts, are you?"

"No! But I was wondering the same about you."

He shook his head. "Uh-uh. I know I argued with you when you wanted to get rid of some stuff, but the truth is, I don't know why I'm hoarding it. I have audiotapes that haven't been played in years, a blender with a blown motor, sets of sheets for a single bed when neither of us actually owns one. I guess I'm just not used to having anyone challenge me over my belongings, my space, and I got my back up. All I really want to hold on to is you."

"That is…so sweet." Emotion throbbed through her and she was horrified that she might make a scene. Yelling at Vi in a dress shop had made her feel like a shrew, to say nothing about fighting with Robert. If she burst into tears now, over enchiladas, it would just be humiliating. She didn't behave this way, so what had happened to her since getting engaged? It was like emotional projectile vomiting. Then again, she and her family had never been closer, as a result of recent emotional honesty.

"Robert, I think some of that stuff, even if you never use it, is important to you because of your parents. I get that a little better now. I wasn't that close to mine before, but a lot's changed."

He gave her a grateful smile.

"You know what we don't have?" she mused aloud. "An engagement picture. I was thinking one would look really good on your parents' mantel. And we should find the perfect spot on our own walls to hang it. It can be our first decoration decision together, unless you don't like the id—"

"I love it." He rose up, leaned over and gave her a quick kiss that promised more as soon as they could get out of there.

A year ago, she might not have welcomed the public show of affection. *Then a year ago, you were an idiot. There's nothing inappropriate about a soon-to-be husband kissing the woman he loves.* Not when she loved him so much. Her father's words came to mind, the obviously deep affection he had for his wife, the certainty that they would always be together, no matter what obstacles they had to overcome to stay that way.

That's what she wanted, that surety and commitment. Even as the rational part of her asked how anyone could be *sure* of anything, she told herself that despite obstacles even the best marriages faced, she was confident she and Robert would try their hardest to make it work.

"Robert? I don't want a prenup."

"What? Are you sure?"

"Getting there." She smiled. "You may not be perfect, Lord knows I'm not, and we'll probably quibble over things. What's important, though, is that you love wholeheartedly and that I'm learning to do the same."

They'd never really fought before the wedding plans, the house hunt, but she was glad now that they'd disagreed. It was good to weather storms together and know that you could come out on the other side even stronger. It was good to express emotions and not be uncomfortable with everything you felt.

He seemed to be at a momentary loss for words.

"Before, I kept a part of myself reserved in all my relationships," she admitted. "Even with my family. I want to change that, not just for you but for myself. I know life doesn't come with guarantees, but can I really live it to the fullest while hedging my bets at the same time? All this moving stuff…I don't want it to be about yours and mine. I just want it to be about us."

"Thank you. You don't know what that means to me."

She studied his face, thought once more about her father's words and how Robert had indeed become her anchor. "Oh, I have an idea."

* * *

Vi leaned against the bar, scribbling the score on a napkin while she waited for the next round of drinks. Currently, she and Phoebe were tied with Savannah and Amanda, Neely's friend from work. Neely and Leah were actually a few points behind, possibly because everyone kept stopping the bride-to-be to congratulate her. This was the third place they'd hit tonight on the bachelorette scavenger hunt Vi had planned, and though Vi had steered clear of any ornamentation that included condoms and phallic symbols, Neely was still noticeable in the crowd with her ivory headband and miniveil.

"So—" Savannah asked as she materialized behind her younger sister "—are there actual prizes for this? Here are the signatures from man wearing a black cowboy hat, woman in spiked heels and member of the band."

Vi smiled. "If there were any prizes, I think Phoebe and I deserve them, don't you? We're *both* single. Neely's snagged one of the last good men, and you're so happy your cheeks probably hurt from all that smiling."

Savannah's ever-present grin widened. "That's me, disgustingly in love as accused."

Thank God. The idea that not even Savannah

could make marriage work had been terrifying, but judging by the bounce in her older sister's step, she and Jason had made a good start on working out their problems. "I'm glad you know." Despite being the family smart aleck and never staying with one man for long, Vi was genuinely thrilled to see her sisters happy.

"I know." Savannah's teasing smile turned affectionate, practically maternal. "Just like we'll all be happy for you when you find the right person."

"Oh, I don't—"

"No hurry," Savannah interrupted. "But maybe someday?"

"Maybe." It had always been Vi's opinion that the beginning of a relationship was the best part, the most fun. Was that only because she'd been scared of what might follow? Neely and Savannah had helped restore the hope it had taken Vi a long time to realize she was missing. True, relationships didn't work out for some people, but Leah and Douglas both seemed to be recovering from their divorces. Though her brother had had some lapses, she wanted to believe him when he said he was finally able to move on. He and Vi had been spending a lot more time together, and it hadn't taken her long to realize his sudden insistence in aiding her home improvement attempts stemmed from wanting something to think about besides Zoe or dating. Vi had become his accountability partner—if he had the urge to call his ex-wife, his sister sent him to Home Depot instead.

Neely made her way to the bar, pausing to acknowledge a few good wishes. "Phoebe sent me to see if the next round had arrived. Leah's dancing with a tall guy in a black cowboy hat. I don't know where we lost Amanda."

"Ladies' room," Savannah said. "I passed her as I was headed this direction. It is starting to get crowded in here, isn't it?"

"If there are too many people," Vi said, "we can go back to my place. I have daiquiri mix and a stack of chick flicks, just in case the scavenger hunt didn't go over well."

"It's been fun," Neely said. "Shockingly enough."

Vi laughed. "You were perhaps expecting male strippers and lewd public displays? Nah, I thought this would be more your style."

"Thank you. Besides, I'm afraid if we go back to your place, you'll put us to work spackling or painting or something." She shuddered. "Moving into my own house has been enough work without transforming yours."

Savannah frowned in Neely's direction, then

turned to Vi. "She's kidding. We're very impressed with the job you've done. I never realized your little duplex could be so adorable."

Vi squirmed, though she wasn't sure why the praise made her uncomfortable. "Well, it was time. Besides, you know how I like change."

Despite her glib tone, she was actually proud of her recent attempts to make something of her life and stop just floating through it. She'd been talking to one of the college counselors about student teaching. Savannah had asked if Vi had any interest in becoming a professor like their father, but Vi thought she'd target a younger age group. Middle school maybe, when kids were starting to hit puberty and some of them were serious brats and others were just neurotic balls of insecurity.

When she'd admitted she was looking into the certification process, Douglas had said he thought she'd be perfect. "You're stubborn and quick thinking. You'd also be harder to intimidate than most, not to mention more caring. You've got a good heart, Vi."

She'd decided that must run in the family.

The ceremony was a blur Neely would never remember in exact detail. The last coherent recollection she had was of her dad hugging her outside the sanctuary, telling her he was happy for her.

"I know some of the people in this family have squawked about how long it took for you to find a husband, but the important thing is that you found the right one, sweet pea. Be happy."

"I will," she vowed, squeezing him back.

Then there'd been the swell of organ music calling her down the aisle, toward Robert and his groomsmen. Savannah, who even managed to make crying delicate and ladylike, had sobbed quiet tears that left her lashes sparkling. Vi, who'd opted to change her hair back to its original color rather than rebleach the roots, stood smiling and radiating a newfound poise. Leah was there, beaming, dateless for the wedding—a decision Douglas had shared, deciding that perhaps he should take a little time for himself.

Neely's friends and family rose, and she swore she could smell the flowers, even though most of the ones in the chapel were fake. The vows passed quickly, with only minor hiccups as she stumbled in a place or two. Did people realize how difficult it was to say "pledge thee my troth"?

Once she and Robert were pronounced man and wife, he gave her a kiss that made her toes curl and she temporarily forgot about everyone watching. Until

Vi cleared her throat and said something under her breath to Savannah that made her giggle.

Neely pulled away from her husband and beamed at the assembled crowd. On the right sat her aunts and parents. On her left, Robert's parents sat in the front row, looking happy if somewhat overwhelmed. During the pictures, Mrs. Walsh had been at a loss for how to respond to Uncle Vernon's ribald jokes and Vi's frank responses when Beth's ordering people about had gotten out of hand. Neely empathized with her new mother-in-law—the Mason family did take some adjusting.

Took me forty-five years, but I got used to them.

Now, the plan was for Robert and Neely to climb into the waiting car in the circular driveway and head for a hotel in downtown Atlanta, where the reception was being held and the newlyweds would spend the night. Neely's first hint that something was up was the sly glance her sisters exchanged; then she thought she glimpsed something bright orange tucked into her brother's cummerbund. So she wasn't entirely surprised when she and Robert emerged through the church doors to find a white car barely visible beneath neon streams of foamy blue, yellow, green and orange Silly String.

She shot a mock glare over her shoulder just in time to see Vi and Douglas high-five.

Robert laughed, shaking his head. "Your siblings are crazy."

"Very true." But they were her kind of crazy, and she wouldn't want them any other way.

* * * * *

You're never too old to sneak out at night

BJ thinks her younger sister, Iris, needs a love interest. So she does what any mature woman would do and organizes an Over-Fifty Singles Night. When her matchmaking backfires it turns out to be the best thing either of them could have hoped for.

Over 50's Singles Night

by Ellyn Bache

Available April 2006
TheNextNovel.com

HN37

There are things inside us
we don't know how to express,
but that doesn't mean
they're not there.

A poignant story about a woman
coming to terms with her relationship
with her father and learning to open up
to the other men in her life.

The Birdman's Daughter

by Cindi Myers

HN38

Available April 2006
TheNextNovel.com

REQUEST YOUR FREE BOOKS!

2 FREE NOVELS TO INTRODUCE YOU TO OUR BRAND-NEW LINE!

NeXt™

There's the life you planned. And there's what comes next.

Detective Maggie Skerritt is on the case again!

Maggie Skerritt is investigating a string of murders while trying to establish her new business with fiancé Bill Malcolm. Can she manage to solve the case while moving on with her life?

Spring*Break*

by *USA TODAY* bestselling author

CHARLOTTE DOUGLAS

You always want
what you don't have

Dinah and Dottie are two sisters who grew up
in an imperfect world. Once old enough to make
decisions for themselves, they went their separate
ways—permanently. Until now. Will their reunion
seventeen years later during a series of crises
finally help them create a perfect life?

My Perfectly
Imperfect Life

Jennifer Archer

If her husband turned up alive—she'd kill him!

The day Fiona Rowland lifted her head above the churning chaos of kids, carpools and errands, annoyance turned to fury and then to worry when she realized Stanley was missing. Can life spiraling out of control end up turning your world upside right?

where's Stanley?

Donna Fasano

Available March 2006
TheNextNovel.com

HN36

A Boca Babe
on a Harley?

Harriet's former life as a Boca Babe—where only
looks, money and a husband count—left her
struggling for freedom. Finally gaining control
of her path, she's leaving that life behind as she
takes off on her Harley. When she drives straight
into a mystery that is connected to her past, will
she be able to stay true to her future?

Dirty Harriet

by Miriam Auerbach

Available April 2006
TheNextNovel.com

HN40

HARLEQUIN®
Next™